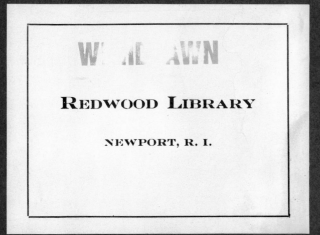

The Late Bourgeois World

Also by Nadine Gordimer

NOVELS

Occasion for Loving
A World of Strangers
The Lying Days

SHORT STORIES

Not for Publication
Friday's Footprint
Six Feet of the Country
The Soft Voice of the Serpent

The Late Bourgeois World

NADINE GORDIMER

New York · The Viking Press

FICTION

The Late Bourgeois World

There are possibilities for me, certainly;
but under what stone do they lie?

—FRANZ KAFKA

The madness of the brave is the wisdom of life.

—MAXIM GORKY

I opened the telegram and said, "He's dead—" and as I looked up into Graham Mill's gaze I saw that he knew who, before I could say. He had met Max, my first husband, a few times, and of course he had heard all about him, he had helped me get to see him when he was in prison. "How?" he said, in his flat professional voice, putting out his hand for the telegram, but I said, "Killed himself!"—and only then let him have it.

It read MAX FOUND DROWNED IN CAR CAPE TOWN HARBOUR. It had been sent by the friend with whom he had probably been staying; I have not heard from Max for more than a year, he didn't even remember Bobo's birthday last month. "Doesn't say when it was," Graham said.

"Last night, or early this morning, must have been." My voice came out cold and angry; I could hear it. It made Graham nervous, he nodded slowly while staring away from me. "Otherwise it would have been in the morning paper. I don't think I looked at the late news—"

The newspaper was on the table among the coffee things. Our cups were half drunk, our cigarettes burned in the saucers; I don't have to go to work on Saturdays, and, as usual, Graham had come to share my late breakfast. We always divide the newspaper, like any old married couple, and the page containing the stop-press column was resting against the honey jar. There was a smear of stickiness on the latest scores in an international golf match: that was all.

Graham, reading over the telegram, said, "Why—I wonder." This was not an unforeseeable end for Max; Graham was questioning what specific demand had brought it about.

I felt immense irritation break out like cold sweat and answered, "Because of me!"

Since I had gone to the door to receive the telegram I had not sat down and stood about like someone stung by insult. Graham patiently bore my angry voice, yet though he must know I spoke in the sense of "to spite me," I saw in his face the astonishing consideration of a self-accusation I had never made, a guilt that, God knows, *he* knew was not mine. Blast him, he chose deliberately to misunderstand me.

He is good about practical matters and he was the first to think of Bobo—"What about the boy? You don't want him to read about it in tonight's paper. Shall I drive over to the school and tell him?" He always refers to Bobo as "the boy"; an expression indicative of formal concern for the sacredness of childhood that amuses me. But I said no, I'd go myself. "The boy" is mine, after all. Perhaps unconsciously —let's be fair to him—Graham tries to move in on responsibility for the child as a means of creating some sort of surety for his relationship with me. It's not for nothing that he has a lawyer's mind. If Bobo starts looking upon any man I'm friendly with as a father, it could be awkward if the friendship were to wane.

"Have some more coffee." Graham filled my cup and patted my chair. But I drank it standing. It was as if I had had a quarrel—but with whom?—and were waiting for the right thing to be said—but by whom? "I'll have to go this morning. I've got to see my grandmother sometime this afternoon." He knows I don't visit the old lady very regularly; "Make it tomorrow." "No, it's her birthday today, I can't." He gave a little parenthetic smile. "How old is she now?"

"Somewhere in the eighties."

I knew exactly how the telegram was worded but I read it over again before crumpling it up and dropping it on the breakfast tray.

While I bathed and dressed Graham sat by the open doors of my balcony, reading the paper with the proper attention it is never given at table. As I went about the flat I kept catching sight of him, his long whipcord-covered legs breaking their knife-crease at the knee, his weekend tweed jacket and clean, old silk shirt, the pale creased jaw and deep eyes, behind glasses, of a man who works late into the nights. Graham has a long mouth whose lips, clearly defined in outline by a change in skin-texture like the milled edge of a coin, are a strange, bluish colour. Under the lights in court, in the fancy dress of a barrister, his face is only the heavy-rimmed glasses and this mouth.

When I was ready to go, he got up to leave the flat, too. "Will you get away from Grandmama in time for a drink at Schroeders'? They're leaving for Europe tomorrow."

"I don't think so."

"What about tonight? Would you like to have dinner somewhere?"

I said, "No, I can't . . . there's some damned dinner party. I can't."

He's not a child, he's forty-six, and he took up his cigarettes and car keys without pique. But as we were leaving the flat I was the one who said, "Could you do something for me? Do you think you could go to a florist and get them to send some flowers to the old lady? Shops'll be closing by the time I get back from the school." He nodded without smiling and wrote down the address in his small, beautiful handwriting.

The road to the school leads away from the hilly ridges of Johannesburg and soon strikes out straight through the mealie fields and flat highveld of the plain. It's early winter; it was one of those absolutely wind-still mornings filled with calm steady sunlight that makes the few trees look black against the pale grass. All that was left of the frost overnight was the fresh smell. There was an old pepper tree here and there, where there must once have been a farmhouse; eucalyptus with tattered curls of bark, twiggy acacias, mud walls of an abandoned hut; an Indian store; a yellowing willow beside a crack in the earth.

It was all exactly as it had been. When I was a child. When Max was a child. It was the morning I had wakened to, gone out into again and again; the very morning. I felt the sun on my eyelids as I drove. How was it possible that it could be still there, just the same, the sun, the pale grass, the bright air, the feeling of it as it was when we had no inkling of what already existed within it. After all that had happened to us, how could this morning, in which nothing had yet happened, still exist? Time is change; we measure its passing by how much things alter. Within this particular latitude of space, which is timeless, one meridian of the sun identical with another, we changed our evil innocence for what was coming to us; if I had gone to live somewhere else in the world I should never have known that this particular morning—phenomenon of geographical position, yearly rainfall, atmospheric pressures—continues, will always continue, to exist.

Max grew up looking out on the veld, here. His parents had their farm—what the estate agents call a country estate—on the edge of the city. His father was a member of parliament and they used to have big Party receptions there. They bred pointers and ducks—for the look of the thing, Max used to say. But he told me that when he was a child he would come back from solitary games in the veld and at a certain point suddenly hear the distant quacking of the ducks like a conversation he couldn't understand.

All this was my way of thinking about Max's death, I suppose, because the fact of his death, even the manner of it, was just something that had been told me. Something to which my contemporary being said quietly: of course. Max had driven a car into the sea and gone down with it; as Max once burned his father's clothes, and, yes, as Max, three years ago, tried to blow up a post office. This time I wasn't looking, that's all. Oh will this child's game never end, between Max and me? *That* was what turned me cold with anger when the telegram came; the feeling that he was looking over the shoulder of his death to see . . . if I were looking?

Perhaps I was flattering myself (dreary flattery, balm that burned like ice, if it was) and there was someone else by now in whose eye he saw himself—friend, woman—it didn't matter whom. But I knew, when I read the telegram, it was *for me*. The worn phrases of human failure, "everything was finished," "broken up," have taken on a new lease of literal meaning between Max and me, we have truly gone through every possibility by which attachment can survive, worn them all threadbare, until any kind of communication was no longer contained, but went like a fist through empty air. And as for broken up—the successive images in which I—we—had seen ourselves together were splintered to crystal dust—like the broken glass, residue of some collision, that I swerved to avoid on the road. But Max would kick from the wreckage the button that asserts the identity of the dead.

The anger left me, then, melted. I always like driving by myself, it brings back something of the self-sufficiency of childhood, and in addition I had the curious freedom of a break in routine. Max was dead; I felt nothing directly about the fact except that I believed it. Yet it divided the morning before I had read the telegram from the morning after I had done so, and in the severance I was cut loose. Of course I can do what I like on Saturday mornings, but it's been weeks since I've done anything but have Graham in to breakfast, wash my hair, and perhaps go to the suburban shops. Even as irregular (in every sense of the word) a thing as this business with Graham and me has taken on a sort of pattern; we go away on holidays together but we don't sleep together often at home—and yet this casualness has become an "arrangement" in itself, and even my evenings in bars and clubs with people he's never heard of are part of habit.

It is also rare for me to get a chance to see Bobo on a Saturday; he's allowed out only twice a month, on Sundays, and the school discourages visits from parents in between times. I realized I hadn't got anything for him. Perhaps they'd let me take him out and I could buy him tea and cream scones at the country hotel near the school. Anyway, I'm the one for whom it is necessary to have presents for Bobo. I see this in his face when I anxiously lay out my carriers of apples and packets of sweets. I know that it is my way of trying to make up for sending him to that place— the school. And yet I had to do it; I have to cover up my reasons by letting it be taken for granted that I want him out of the way. For the truth is that I would hold on to Bobo, if I let myself. I could keep him clamped to my belly like one of those female baboons who carry their young clinging beneath their bodies. And I would never let go.

I can't give him the life with the indispensable units, a mother and father and family, I was taught was a sacred trust to provide for any child I might "bring into the world." I'm not even sure it would be enough, either, if I could. I had that life, Max had it, and yet it hasn't seemed to have provided what it turned out we needed. Oh I know it's easy enough to blame our parents for our troubles, and we belong to the generation that lays down its burdens on Freud, as our parents were exhorted to lay down theirs on Jesus. But I don't think that the code of decent family life,

kindness to dogs and neighbours, handouts to grateful servants, has brought us much more than bewilderment. What
about all those strangers the code didn't provide for, the
men who didn't feel themselves to be our servants and had
nothing to be grateful for in being fobbed off with handouts, the people who weren't neighbours and crowded in on
us with hurts and hungers kindness couldn't appease? I
don't know what will be asked of Bobo by the time he
grows up, but I do know that the sort of background I was
told a child should expect would leave him pretty helpless.
I can only try to see to it that he looks for this kind of security elsewhere than in the white suburbs.

He wasn't made there, thank God. It was in a car—which
is where the white suburbs keep their sex. But at least it
was out in the veld. One of the millions of babies made in
cars, plantations, parks, alleys, all over the world. Because
the suburbs, while talking romantic rubbish about "the
young people" among the flowers and decanters of the living room, ignore sex, the defining need of their youth.
There are bedrooms, studies, dens, porches; but no place
for that. I said to Max, "You forgot." He shrugged gloom-
ily, as if he had never promised. But I knew it was my
"fault" as much as his. Then he said, speaking without any
relation to circumstances, as he often did, I'd like to have a
child of my own. I'd like to have a child following me
round, there's nothing doggy about children. A child shouts
'Look!' all the time and you see real things, colours of
stones, and bits of wood." The last time he saw Bobo was
more than a year ago. I could see that he liked him better
than when he was little and used to yell; I was pleased that
he could fool with him and forget that he used to yell back

until the child's open mouth went soundless with fright and I had to take him away and carry him round the streets.

Just before I reached the school there was one of those lorries that sell fruit at the side of the road, and a black man jumped up from a little fire he'd made himself and pranced out with an orange stuck on a stick. I bought a packet of nartjies for Bobo.

The school has very large grounds with a small dam and a plantation of eucalyptus trees—that was one of the reasons why I chose it: so that he would have somewhere that at least he could pretend was wild, to get away to from playing fields and corridors. It's difficult to remember what it was like being a child, but I do know that it was essential to have such a place. The buildings (and the gateposts with their iron arch bearing the school crest, and name in Celtic lettering) are of yellow brick that breaks out in crosses, raised like Braille bumps, all over the place. The sight of the school produces a subdued and cowed mood in me; I go on mental tiptoe from the moment I enter that gateway. Black men in neat overalls are always busy in the grounds trimming the hedges at sharp right-angles and digging round the formal beds and clipped shrubs; they were sweeping up leaves, this time. Tin signs cut in the shape of a hand with pointing forefinger and painted in the headmaster's wife's Celtic lettering, indicate "Visitors' Parking," "Staff Only," "Office." The whole curve of the drive before the main building was empty but in the subservient anxiousness to do right that comes over me, I left the car in the visitors' parking ground. It was about eleven o'clock and the cries of the boys at break came from the quadrangles and playing fields behind the buildings. I know that my view of the place is absurdly subjective, but how like a prison it was! Behind the clean and ugly bricks, a great shout of life going up, fading into the sunlit vacuum. I went up the polished steps and dropped the heavy knocker on the big oiled door.

It was opened by what must have been a new junior master, heavy-jawed, nice-looking, with the large, slightly shaky hands, powerful but helpless, of the young man who is going through the stage of intense desire for women without knowing how to approach any. He wore shabby, fashionably narrow-legged pants and a knitted tie and was obviously one of the Oxford or Cambridge graduates working their way round Africa who are counted on to bring a healthy blast of contemporaneity into the curriculum. (Bobo has told me about one who played the guitar and taught the boys American antibomb and antisegregation folk songs.)

The headmaster was at tea in the staff room, but the young man took me to the headmaster's study and asked me to sit down while he fetched him. I've been in that study a number of times; hostilely clean, hung with crossed-armed athletic groups, the shiny brown plastic flooring covered with a brown carpet in the standard concession to comfort to be found in the rooms of administrators of institutions. There was even a framed cartoon of the headmaster, cut from the school magazine; everyone said what an "approachable," "human" man he was.

He said how nice it was to see me—just as if one could drop in to the school any old time, instead of being sternly discouraged from appearing outside the prescribed visiting days. And although he must have known I had something serious to say, his quick, peg-on-the-nose voice dealt out a succession of pleasantries that kept us both hanging fire. But no doubt the poor devil dreads parents' problems, and this is just an unconscious device to stave off their recital. I told him that Bobo's father had died, and how. He was understanding and sensible, according to the manual of appropriate behaviour for such an occasion, but in his face with its glaze of artificial attentiveness there was certainty of his distance from people like us. He knew the circumstances of Bobo's background; divorce, political imprisonment, and now this. He knew it all the way, as a broad-minded man and a good Christian, I suppose he follows in the papers the Church's self-searching over homosexuality or abortion. He and Mrs. Jellings, who teaches art at the school, must have been married for at least twenty-five years, and last year their daughter was married from the school with a guard of honour of senior boys.

He got up and opened the door and stopped a boy who was passing in the corridor. "Braithwaite! Send Bruce Van Den Sandt here, will you? D'you know him? He's in fourth." "Yes sir, I know Van Den Sandt, sir. I think he's on library duty." And he skidded off in a way that automatically drew a quick dent between the headmaster's eyebrows.

Bruce Van Den Sandt. I hardly ever hear the name spoken. This is the other Bobo, whom I will never know. Yet it always pleases me to hear it; a person in his own right, complete, conjured up in himself. It was Max's name; Max was dead, but like a word passed on, his name was called aloud in the school corridor.

The headmaster said, "Come in here. I suppose you'll want to talk to him alone; that'll be best." And he opened a door I'd seen, but never been through before, marked "Visitors' Room." I'd cowardly lost the moment to say, "I'd

like to take him out and talk to him while we drive."
Why am I idiotically timid before such people, while at the
same time so critical of their limitations?

I sat in this shut-up parlour whose purpose I had now
gained entry to and waited quite a little while before the
door flung open and he filled the doorway—Bobo. He had
the glowing ears and wide nostrils of a boy brought from
the middle of a game, his hands were alert to the catch, his
clothes were twisted, his smile was a grin of breathlessness.
The high note of this energy might, like a certain pitch in
music, have silently shattered the empty vase and the glass
on the engravings of Cape scenes.

"Ma? Well, nobody told me you were coming!"

He hugged me and we giggled, as we always do with the
glee of being together and clandestine to school and everything else.

"How'd you get in?"

I hadn't thought about what I was going to say to Bobo,
and now it was too late. I gripped his hand and gestured
hard with it in mine, once or twice, to call us to attention,
and said, "We've got to talk, Bo. Something about Max,
your father."

At once he caught me out, as if he were the adult and I
the child. He understood that I never referred to Max as
anyone but "Max." He was little when Max was on trial
and in prison, but I have told him all about it since he's
been older. He nodded his head with a curious kind of
acceptance. He knows there is always the possibility of trouble.

We sat down together on the awful little settee, like lovers facing each other for a declaration in a Victorian illus-

tration. He dragged at his collapsed socks—"Pull your socks up, your mother's here, Jelly said."

"He died, Bobo. They sent me a telegram this morning. It'll be in the papers, so I must tell you—he killed himself."

Bobo said, "You mean he committed suicide?"

Amazement smoothed and widened his face, the flush left it except for two ragged patches, like the scratches of some animal, on the lower cheeks. What came to him in that moment must have been the reality of all the things he had read about, happening to other people, the X showing where on the pavement the body fell, the arrow pointing at the blurred figure on the parapet.

I said, "Yes," and to blot it all out, once and for all, to confine it, "He must have driven his car into the sea. He was never afraid of the sea, he was at home in it."

He nodded, but he kept his eyes wide open on me, the brows, over their prominent frontal ridge, scrolled together in concentration. What was he facing? The fact of his own death? Mine? Bobo and I didn't have to pretend to each other that we were grieving over Max in a personal way. If you haven't had a father, can you lose him? Bobo hardly knew him; and although I hadn't, couldn't explain all that to him, he knows that I had come to the end of knowing Max.

Bobo said, "I somehow just can't see his face."

"But it's not so long since you saw him. Eighteen months, not more."

"I know, but then I hardly remembered what he looked like at all, and I was looking at him all the time the way you do with a new person. Then afterwards you can't see their face."

"You've got a photograph, though." There on his locker, the upright leather folder with mother on one side, father on the other, just as all the other boys have.

"Oh yes."

There didn't seem to be anything else to say; at least, not all at once, and not in that room.

"I brought you some nartjies. I forgot to get anything in town."

He said absently, making the show of pleasure that is his form of loving politeness, "Mmm . . . thanks. But I won't take them now . . . just before you go, so's when I've seen you off I can stick them in my desk before anyone sees."

Then he said, "Let's go outside for a bit," and when I said, "But are we allowed to? I wanted to ask Mr. Jellings—" "—Really, Mummy, what's there to be so chicken about? I don't know how you'd manage in this joint!" As we closed the door of the visitors' room behind us, I said, "We've never been in there, before." "It's for long-distance parents, really, though I don't know what it's *for*—you can tell from the pong no one ever goes in there." I smiled at the jargon. Bobo has mastered everything; that place has no terrors for him.

We kept to the formal, deserted front garden, away from the other boys. We walked up and down, talking trivialities, like people in hospital grounds who are relieved to have left the patient behind for a while. Bo told me he had written to me asking for new soccer boots, and whether it would be all right if Lopert came home with him next Sunday. I'd had a circular from the school about boxing lessons, and wanted to know if Bo were interested. Then we went to sit in the car, and he teased, "Why'n't you just park in town and walk, Ma?"

Like most boys Bobo has a feeling for cars akin to the sense of place, and when he gets into the car I can see that it's almost as if he were home, in the flat. He noses through all the old papers that collect on the shelf beneath the dashboard and looks for peppermints and traffic tickets in the glove box. I am often called upon to explain myself.

He was sitting beside me touching a loose knob, probably noting with some part of his mind that he must fix it sometime, and he said, "I don't suppose it was painful or anything."

I said, "Oh no. You mustn't worry about that." Because all his life, he's been made aware of the necessity to recognize and alleviate suffering; it's the one thing he's been presented with as being beyond questioning, since the first kitten was run over and the first street beggar was seen displaying his sores.

"Just the idea." His head was low; now he looked round towards me without lifting it, sideways, and I knew quite well that what he was really asking about was the unknown territory of adult life where one would choose to die. But I wasn't equal to that. He was. He blurted, "I feel sorry I didn't love him."

I looked at him without excuses. The one thing I hope to God I'll never do is fob him off with them.

I said, "There may be talk among the boys—but you know he went after the right things, even if perhaps it was in the wrong way. The things he tried didn't come off but at least he didn't just eat and sleep and pat himself on the back. He wasn't content to leave bad things the way they are. If he failed, well, that's better than making no attempt. Some boys' "—I was going to say "fathers" but I didn't want him to go attacking all the scions of stockbroking houses—"some men live successfully in the world as it is, but they don't have the courage even to fail at trying to change it."

He looked satisfied. He is only a child, after all; he said with a rough sigh, "We've had a lot of trouble through politics, haven't we."

"Well, we can't really blame this on politics. I mean, Max suffered a lot for his political views, but I don't suppose this—what he did now—is a *direct* result of something political. I mean—Max was in a mess, he somehow couldn't deal with what happened to him, largely, yes, because of his political actions, but also because . . . in general, he wasn't equal to the demands he . . . he took upon himself." I added lamely, "As if you insisted on playing in the first team when you were only good enough—strong enough for third."

As he followed what I was saying his head moved slightly in the current from the adult world, the way I have sometimes noticed a plant do in a breath of air I couldn't feel.

In the end he has to take on trust what he is told; the only choice he can exercise is *by whom*. And he chooses me. At times I'm uneasy to see how sceptically he reports what he is told by others. But the reaction will come with adolescence, if I'm to believe what *I've* been told is "healthy development." He'll tear me down. But with what? Of course I'd craftily like to find out, so that I can defend myself in advance, but one generation can never know the weapons of the next. He picked up my hand and kissed it swiftly on the back near the thumb just as he used to do suddenly, for no reason I knew, when he was little. It must be five years since he stopped doing it, out of embarrassment or because he didn't need to. But there was no one to see, in the empty car park. He said, "What are you going to do today? Is Graham coming over?"

"I don't think so. I saw him this morning, he was there for breakfast."

"I expect Jellings'll put Max in prayers tonight. Usually when a relation dies he's in prayers."

So Max would have a service for his soul in the school chapel. There wouldn't be any other. It wasn't likely they'd pray for him, the ones he worked with, the ones he betrayed. Max wasn't anybody's hero; and yet, who knows? When he made his poor little bomb it was to help blow the blacks free; and when he turned State witness the whites, I suppose, might have taken it as justification for claiming him their own man. He may have been just the sort of hero we should expect.

I've noticed that Bobo always senses when I am about to go. He said, "Let me turn the car for you?" and I didn't dare suggest that he might get into trouble if anyone saw him, but obediently moved over to the passenger seat as he got out and came round to the driver's side. He drove once right round the parking ground and then I said, "That's enough. Hop out." He laughed and pulled a face and put the brake on. "See you Sunday week, then. And you're bringing whatsisname—"

"Lopert."

"I don't think I've met him, have I? What about Weldon, doesn't he want to come too?" Weldon is another of the boys who live too far away to be able to go home on Sunday outings; all last term Bobo brought him to the flat.

"I expect he'll be going with the Pargiters."

"Have you two quarrelled or something?"

"No, well, he's always talking about 'munts' and things

—and when we get hot after soccer he says we smell like
kaffirs. Then when I get fed up he thinks it's because I'm
offended at him saying *I'm* like a kaffir—he just doesn't understand that it's not that at all, what I can't stand is him
calling them kaffirs and talking as if they were the only ones
who ever smell. He just laughs and is as nice as anything.
. . . He doesn't understand. There's nothing wrong in it, to
him. Nearly all the boys are like that. You get to like them
a hell of a lot, and then they say things. You just have to
keep quiet." He was looking at me frowningly, his face
stoical, dismayed, looking for an answer but knowing, already, there wasn't one. He said, "Sometimes I wish we
were like other people."

I said, "What people?"

"They don't care."

"I know." In full view of blank school buildings we exchanged the approved cheek-kiss expected of mothers and
sons. "Next Sunday."

"Don't be late. Don't forget to get up, the way you always
do."

"Ne-ver! —The nartjies!" He turned back for me to
thrust the paper carrier through the window, and I saw him
career off up the drive with the bulge buttoned under his
blazer, feet flying, whorl of hair sticking up on the crown. I
felt, as I sometimes do, an unreasonable confidence in
Bobo. He is all right. He will be all right.

In spite of everything.

*F*rom a long way off the city on a Saturday sounded the roar of a giant shell pressed against my ear. I had absently taken a wrong turning on the way back and approached by a route that went through one of the new industrial areas that are making the country rich—or rather, richer. Caterpillar tractors were grouped as statuary in the landscaped gardens of the factory that made them. For more than a mile I was stuck behind a huge truck carrying bags of coal and the usual gang of delivery men, made blacker by gleaming coal-dust, braced against the speed of the truck round a blazing brazier. They always look like some cheerful scene out of hell, and don't seem to care tuppence about the proximity of the petrol tank. Then when I got into the suburbs I had another truck ahead of me, loaded with carefully padded "period" furniture to which black men clung with precarious insouciance. They didn't care a damn, either. There was a young one with a golfer's cap pulled down over his eyes who held on by one hand while he used the other to poke obscene gestures at the black girls. They laughed back or ignored him; no one seemed outraged. But when he caught my smile he looked right through me as though I wasn't there at all.

In a suburban shopping centre I stopped to pick up cigarettes and something from the delicatessen. I had a cup of coffee in a place that had tables out on the pavement among tubs of frost-bitten tropical shrubs. It was almost closing time for the shops and the place was crowded with young women in expensive trousers and boots, older women in elegant suits and furs newly taken out of storage, men in the rugged weekend outfit of company directors, and demanding children shaping icecream with their tongues. A woman at the table I was sharing was saying, ". . . I've made a little list . . . he hasn't got a silver cigarette case, you know, for one thing . . . I mean, when he goes out in the evening, to parties, he really needs one."

And when he goes down to the bottom of the sea? Will he need a silver cigarette case there?

She was exactly like Max's mother, pink-and-white as good diet and cosmetics could make her, the fine lines of her capacity to be amused crinkling her pretty blue eyes, her rose fingernails moving confidently. She even had Mrs. Van Den Sandt's widow's peak that showed up so well in the big pastel that hung above the fireplace in the yellow sitting room. How she impressed me the first time Max took me to the farm, when I was seventeen! She was so charming, and I had not known that everyday life could be made so pretty and pleasant. The cupboards were scented and the bathrooms had fluffy rugs and tall flagons of oils and colognes that anyone could use. ("Yes," Max said, "my mother puts a frilly cover over everything; the lavatory seat, her mind—") You could have your clothes pressed or ring for a glass of fresh orange juice or tea or coffee any time you liked. There were menservants in starched white with red sashes to whom Mrs. Van Den Sandt spoke Xhosa, and a Cape Coloured cook with whom Mrs. Van Den Sandt talked Afrikaans, using all the wheedling diminutives and terms of respect of the Cape patois. "I know these people as if they were my own," she would say, when guests remarked that they envied her her excellent servants. "I was brought up among them. I can still remember how the natives used to come from miles around to visit my mother. There was one old man, supposed to have once been a headman of Sandile, the Gaika chief, he used to come once a month regularly. He would sit under the *ysterhout* tree and my mother would bring him a mug of coffee with her own hands. I can see it now."

She was the descendant of an old Cape Dutch family who had intermarried with English-speaking people, and had served at various South African embassies in Europe. Although her quick, light speech was sprinkled with the "darlings" of fashionable English women of her generation, she kept a slight Afrikaans intonation here and there, as a French *diseuse* who has been performing for years in English is careful not to lose entirely the quaint distinction of her accent. People also found it beguiling when she gave the lie, with naïve, playful pride, to her English "county" appearance—the sweaters and pearls—by saying stoutly, simply, "I'm a Boer girl, you know. I must go out and get my feet dirty among the mealies now and then." Max's father —despite the Flemish name—came from an English family that emigrated to South Africa when the gold mines started up. He was a small man with a big red face shining as if it had been left to dry without being towelled, stiff hair varnished back flat to his head in one piece, and a cleft chin. He had the gift of being particularly friendly towards people whom he disliked or feared, and, with one short stiff arm up on the shoulder of a political rival on either side of him, would go off into chesty laughter at the anecdote he was telling.

Even that first time I went to the house there were people there. There were always parties or bridge evenings— gatherings of people it was necessary to entertain, rather than friends—or meetings that ended with the drinks and snacks being carried through the cigar smoke by Jonas and Alfred wearing their red sashes. Later, when I became a regular visitor to the house, Mrs. Van Den Sandt would descend on us from the chattering, drinking, eating company: "The children, the children! Come and have some food!" But after we'd shouldered our way in among the behinds in black cocktail dresses and the paunches in pinstripe, and had been introduced to a few people here and there: "Of course you know Max, my son? And this is little Elizabeth—eat something, my pet, Max, you *don't* look after this girl, she looks pinched—" we were forgotten. The talk of stocks and shares, the property market, the lobbying for support for Bills that would have the effect of lowering or raising the bank rate, on which they depended for their investments, industrial Bills on which they depended for

cheap labour, or land apportionment on which they depended to keep the best for themselves—all this grew together in a thicket of babble outside which we finished our
plates of chicken *en gêlée* and silently drank our glasses of
chilled white wine. Max had grown up in that silence; the
babble was perhaps what he heard in the distant conversation of the ducks, when he approached the farm alone over
the veld.

I say of the Van Den Sandts that they "were" this or that;
but, of course, they *are*. Somewhere in the city while I was
drinking my coffee, Mrs. Van Den Sandt, with her handbag
filled, like the open one of the woman sitting beside me,
with grown-up toys—the mascot key-ring, the tiny gilt pen-
cil, the petit-point address book, the jewelled pill-box—was
learning that Max was dead—again. Their son was dead for
them the day he was arrested on a charge of sabotage. Theo
Van Den Sandt resigned his seat in Parliament, and he
never came to court, though he made money available for
Max's defence. She came several times. We sat there on the
white side of the public gallery, but not together. One day,
when her hair was freshly done, she wore a fancy lace man-
tilla instead of a hat that would disturb the coiffure. Her
shoes and gloves were perfectly matched and I saw with fas-
cination that some part of her mind would attend to these
things as long as she lived, *no matter what happened*. She
sat rigidly upright on the hard bench with her mascaraed
eyelashes lowered almost to her cheeks, and never once
looked round, not at the rest of us on the white side, wives
and mothers and friends of the white accused (Max was
charged with accomplices) with our parcels of food that we
were allowed to provide for their lunch every day, nor to

her left, across the barrier, where old black men in broken overcoats and women with their bundles sat in patience like a coiled spring.

At the recess as we all clattered into the echoing corridors of the courts, I smelt her perfume. People talking as they went, forming groups that obstructed each other, had squeezed us together. The jar of coming face to face opened her mouth after years of silence between us. She spoke. "What have we done to deserve this!" Under each eye and from lips to chin were deep scores, the lashes of a beauty's battle with age. I came back at her—I don't know where it came from—"You remember when he burned his father's clothes."

Footsteps rang all about us, we were being jostled.

"What? All children get up to things. That was nothing."

"He did it because he was in trouble at school, and he'd tried to talk about it to his father for days, but his father was too busy. Every time he tried to lead round to what he wanted to say he was told, run away now, your father's busy."

Her painted mouth shaped an incredulous laugh. "What are you talking about."

"Yes, you don't remember. But you'll remember it was the time when your husband was angling to get into the Cabinet. The time when he wanted to be Chief Whip, and was so busy."

I was excited with hatred of her self-pity, the very smell of her stank in my nostrils. Oh we bathed and perfumed and depilated white ladies, in whose wombs the sanctity of the white race is entombed! What concoction of musk and boiled petals can disguise the dirt done in the name of that sanctity? Max took that dirt upon himself, tarred and feathered himself with it, and she complained of her martyred respectability. I wanted to wound her; could nothing wound her? She turned her back as one does on someone of whom it is useless to expect anything.

And yet, at the beginning, the Van Den Sandts regarded me as an ally. Not personally, but in my capacity as a "normal" interest for a boy who didn't have many. If their Max wouldn't join the country club or pull his weight as a member of the United Party Youth, then at least he'd found himself a "little girl." The "little" was used as indicative of my social standing, not my size; I was a shopkeeper's daughter from a small town, while Max's father not only had been a front bencher in the Smuts government but was also a director of various companies, from cigarette manufacture to plastic packaging. When Max was a student they didn't take him very seriously, of course, and regarded what they knew of his activities in student politics, along with his pointed nonappearance at dinner parties and his shabby clothes, as youthful Bohemianism. I don't know whether they ever knew that he was a member of a Communist cell; probably not. To them it was all a game, a fancy dress ball like the ones *they* used to go to in the Thirties. Soon he would put away the costume, wear a suit, join one of his father's companies, invest in the share market, and build a nice home for the little girl he would marry. They had no idea that he was spending his time with African and Indian students who took him home where he had never been before, to the Locations and ghettoes, and introduced him to men who, while they worked as white men's drivers and cleaners and factory hands, had formulated their own views of their destiny and had their own ideas of setting about to achieve it. For the Van Den Sandts none of this existed; when Mrs. Van Den Sandt spoke of "we South Africans" she meant the Afrikaans and English-speaking white people, and when Theo Van Den Sandt called for "a united South Africa, going forward to an era of progress and prosperity for all" he meant the unity of the same two white groups, and higher wages and bigger cars for them. For the rest—the ten or eleven million "natives"—their labour was directed in various Acts of no interest outside Parliament, and their lives were incidental to their labour, since until the white man came they knew nothing better than a mud hut in the veld. As for the few who had managed to get an education, the one or two outstanding ones who were let in to the University alongside her own son—Mrs. Van Den Sandt thought it "marvellous, how some of them can raise themselves if they make the effort"; but the "effort" was not related in her mind to any room in a Location yard where somebody else's son puzzled through his work by the light of a bit of candle, squashing with his thumbnail (I always remember this description of his student days given by one of our friends) the bugs as they crawled out of their cracks.

The Van Den Sandts must have relied on me to lead Max by the penis, as it were, into the life he was born for; and I suppose that was why she was inclined to take with sophisticated tolerance, unlike my own parents, the fact that I got myself pregnant at eighteen. "It's just a *mistake,* that's all," she said in a sort of soothing baby-talk, as if a puppy had wet the carpet. And after Max and I were married she looked at me with mock censure, raising her eyebrows and smiling when we came to lunch one day: "Oh *look* at its little belly, if you please! My dear, all the old cats are going to start counting soon—but we don't care a fig for them, do we!"

Max's face changed and without greeting her he turned and went out of the room. I found him in his old bedroom. "If I don't bother about it, why should you?" But what was a silly incident, to me, was the ruthless persistence of a social manner that had affectionately belittled him, all his life. Only a man could beget a child, yet she managed to make it something "clever" and "naughty" the children had done.

It was while I was pregnant, in 1952, that the Defiance Campaign began. Max was one of a group of white people who marched into an African area prohibited to whites, and he also went to Durban to camp with Africans and Indians on a public square in protest against segregation. Of course, the whole idea was to get oneself arrested and to go to jail. But the charges against Max were dropped, and although we never found out why, he was always convinced that his father had contrived it. If this was so, it was a terrible thing to do to Max; but of course they didn't do it for Max, they did it for themselves. It wouldn't have done for a prominent United Party M.P. to have a son in prison for defiance of colour bar laws, even though by that time the Nationalists had been in power for five years and Van Den Sandt had lost for good his chance of becoming a Cabinet minister. If Max wouldn't act as a white man for white men, the Van Den Sandts wouldn't let him act at all. That's what they wanted to do to him. And then a time came when he made a bomb.

They were gathering together their weekend purchases

all round me, the good citizens who never had any doubt about where their allegiance lay. The steady winter sun, so bone-warming, so reassuringly benign (perhaps we can't help feeling that if we have the best climate in the world we must deserve it?) shone on the shapes of bottles of wine and whisky, the prawns and cakes and bunches of flowers, plain evidence of the superior living standards of white civilization, that they were taking home. I saw them give their children pennies to drop into the S.P.C.A. collection box and the hat of the black beggar. Home-made bombs have not shaken the ground under their feet, nor have the riots, the marches, the shootings of a few years back, though like all decent people, they deplore the inhumanity of violence, and, reserving the right of constitutional action to themselves alone, commend it to others as the only decent way to achieve change—should one want such a thing.

I too have my package of pork fillets and my chair in the sun; you would not know me from the others. We are all still alive and the cars are crawling impatiently one behind the other. Whereas Max is in the sea, in the soup, at the bottom of the sea; poor madman: I suppose it will be possible to say that, now, as it has been satisfactorily possible to say, in the end, of many who have proved awkward, including the one who didn't know that a Prime Minister with a divine mission might need a silver bullet. Only madmen do such things. But can any white man who wants change really be all there? It's a comforting thought.

Some of them would remember, today, that they were right not to take Max seriously, poor devil, when he made that frightful speech at his sister's wedding. If they were castigated, well, the poor fellow was unbalanced. It was

long before the bomb, Lord yes, long before it had come to
that—long before we had come to a lot of things. Max and
I were still together, Bobo was a little baby a few months
old, we still, curiously, had some sort of place in the Van
Den Sandt family life. It was after the Defiance Campaign
affair, of course, but I suppose since Max's part in that had
been hushed up, the Van Den Sandts didn't feel that that
constituted a valid rift between Max and themselves. Only
public injury counts, with them. In one of those twists of an
ancient code degenerating far from its source that is charac-
teristic of a civilization brought over the sea and kept in
mothballs, the Van Den Sandts interpret honour as something that exists in the eyes of others; you can do each other
to death, in private: shame or pain come only from what
leaks out. A daughter's wedding to a suitable candidate was
a public occasion (they'd been done out of Max's by my
pregnancy even if Max would not have refused to play) and
the bride's only brother was a traditional participant in the
jocular clannish emotionalism of the celebration. Therefore
Max lost all other identity; the Van Den Sandts insisted
that he must propose the toast to Queenie and her bride-
groom. I think they felt confident that the convention of
the occasion would carry him along as such things did for
them, through everything; that, married, with a wife and
baby of his own, the ceremonies and loyalties of his kind
would hold sway over him at last, he would "rise to it" irresistibly, like the good fellow any son of theirs *must be,* underneath, after all.

I was surprised that Max gave in; I had wondered if I'd
be able to get him to go to the wedding at all. I thought it
must be because of Queenie, of whom he was fond, in an

unthinking sort of way—she was so pretty, one of those girls whom one sets aside in one's mind from any further necessity to account for themselves.

"What on earth will you find to say?" I asked, laughing at the idea of him.

"As if you're expected to *say* anything," he said. "To the happy couple!"

And I waved an imaginary glass and responded, "Yay! Hurray!"

Mrs. Van Den Sandt gave me money to buy myself a dress for the wedding; a generous gift, spoilt by her inability to resist the remark: "Don't let Theo know how much your little dress cost—he'll be furious at my extravagance!" so that I'd be sure to understand how generous she had been and how modest my expectations of the Van Den Sandts ought to be. What she didn't know was that the dress cost less than half of what I told her, and I'd used the rest of the money to pay the chemist and dairy. I sat there behind the swag of carnations and roses that decorated the bride's table, eating smoked salmon and drinking champagne, and felt only an empathetic inward trill of shyness—hidden by the smile politely exchanged with the uncle next to me—when Max got up to speak. Max is—was—slight and not very tall, but he had the big wrists and the small bright blue, far-sighted eyes of his mother's antecedents; in him, unmistakably, was the Boer identity that she archly claimed for herself. He wore his dark suit and his best, raw silk tie that I had given him. He gave, to the expanse of tablecloth directly beneath him rather than anywhere else, the nervous smile that always reminded me of the mouth-movement of an uncertain feline animal, not snarling, unable to express a greeting, yet acknowledging an approach. He did not look at me, nor at anyone. His first few words were lost in the talk that had not quite yet damped down, but then his voice emerged, ". . . my sister and Allan, the man she has chosen to marry, a happy life together. Naturally we wish them this, though there's not much more we can do about it than wish. I mean it's up to them."

There was a stir towards laughter, a false start—they were expecting to have to respond to a joke or innuendo soon, but Max did not seem to understand, and went on, "I don't know Allan at all, and although I think I know my sister, I don't suppose I know much about her, either. We have to leave it to them to make a go of it for themselves. And—good luck to them. They're young, my sister's beautiful—"

And this time the growl of laughter was confident. Max became inaudible, though I guessed he was probably saying something about the beauty being in spite of the way she'd been got up for the day. The guests had decided that his ignoring of their response was some sort of dead-pan wit and their laughter surged appreciatively into every pause or hesitation as he went on, ". . . between the two of them. But the kind of life they'll live, the way they'll live among other people—that's another thing again, and here one can have something to say. I know I'm supposed to be speaking for everybody here" (there was an emotional murmur of support) "—all these people who have known Queen since she was born, and who have known her husband, known Allan—and who have come here full of the good feeling they get when they get together and drink each other's health—your health, Queen and Allan—but I'd like to say off my own bat" (eyes were on him with the indulgent, smiling attention good manners decreed) "don't let the

world begin and end for you with the—how many is it?
four hundred?—people sitting here in this—the Donnybrook Country *and Sporting* Club today. These good
friends of our parents and Allan's parents, our father's
regional chairman and the former ministers of this and that
(I don't want to make a mistake in the portfolios) and all
the others, I don't know the names but I recognize the
faces, all right—who have made us, and made this club, and
made this country what it is." (There was prolonged clapping, led by someone with loud, hard palms.) "There's a
whole world outside this." (Applause broke out again.)
"Shut outside. Kept out. Shutting this in. . . . Don't stay
inside and let your arteries harden, like theirs . . . I'm not
talking about the sort of thing some of them have, those
who have had their thrombosis, I don't mean veins gone
furry through sitting around in places like this fine club
and having more than enough to eat—" (clapping began
and spattered out, like mistaken applause between movements at a concert) "What I'm asking you to look out for
is—is moral sclerosis. Moral sclerosis. Hardening of the
heart, narrowing of the mind; while the dividends go up.
The thing that makes them distribute free blankets in the
Location in winter, while refusing to pay wages people
could live on. Smugness. Among us, you can't be too young
to pick it up. It sets in pretty quick. More widespread than
bilharzia in the rivers, and a damned side harder to cure."

There was a murmurous titter. The uncle beside me
whispered anxiously, "He's inherited his father's gifts as a
speaker."

"It's a hundred-per-cent endemic in places like this
Donnybrook Country *and Sporting* Club, and in all the
suburbs you're likely to choose from to live in. Just don't be

too sure they're healthy, our nice clean suburbs for whites only."

They were smiling blindly, deafly, keeping their attitudes of bland attention as they would have done if the hostess had lost her panties on the dance floor, or they had suddenly overheard an embarrassing private noise.

"—and your children. If you have babies, Queenie and Allan, don't worry too much about who kisses them—it's what they'll tell them, later, that infects. It's what being nicely brought up will make of them that you've got to watch out for. Moral sclerosis—yes, that's all I wanted to say, just stay alive and feeling and thinking—and that's all I can say that'll be of any use . . ."

Max suddenly became aware of the people about him, and sat down. There was a second of silence and then the same pair of hard palms began to clap and a few other hands followed hollowly, but someone at the bride's table at once leapt up and thrust out his glass in the toast that Max had forgotten—"The bride and groom!" All the gilded folding chairs shuffled and all the figures rose in solidarity—"To the bride and groom!" I saw the determinedly smiling faces behind the glasses of wine as if they had turned on him. But the voices of congratulation clashed over my head, the band struck up "For They Are Jolly Good Fellows," and the din swept over him, ignoring him, asserting them. In a little while nobody seemed to remember that the speech had been any different from dozens of others they'd sat through and didn't remember. Only Mrs. Van Den Sandt's make-up stood out like a face drawn on her face as she leant vivaciously across the table to receive kisses and congratulations; the skin beneath must have been drained of blood.

Poor Max—*moral sclerosis!* The way he fell in love with
that prig's phrase and kept repeating it: *moral sclerosis.*
Where on earth had he got it from? And all the analogies
he kept raking up to go with it. Like our old Sunday school
lessons—the world is God's garden and we are all His flowers, etc. (The Blight of Dishonesty, Aphids of Doubt.) And
could there have been a more unsuitable time and place for
such an attempt? What sort of show could his awkward
honesty make against sheer rudeness of him? *They* were all
in the right, again, and he was wrong; and I could have
kicked him for it. We did not leave the wedding. We stayed
on and got rather tight and danced together in an ostenta-
tious solidarity of our own, but I couldn't say a word to him
about the speech, it was so horribly funny, and I suppose
that made him ashamed, and he sulked for days.

As for the bride, his sister Queenie, home and school had
succeeded with her so completely that she did not understand his strange, muddled outburst sufficiently to feel the
need to ignore it. "What a jawing to give us at our wedding!" she complained good-naturedly. "I thought I was
back at school or something! You think because you got
married first you can lecture me like an old grandpa!"

Moral sclerosis; good God.

After all this time, the idiotic term still makes me
squirm—and apparently express the embarrassment out-
wardly, in a smile: when I drew up before the raised glove
of the traffic policeman who's on duty at my corner on Saturdays, I realized that he was smiling back at the female behind glass in the manner of one responding to the unex-
pected, but never unwelcome overture.

The telephone was ringing as I came into the flat, but when I reached it, it stopped. I was sure it was Graham and then I saw a bunch of flowers under cellophane, on the table; he'd got the florist to send them here instead of to the Home. But my name was on the finicky little envelope—he had sent me flowers at the same time as he ordered them for the old lady. Samson the cleaner must have been working in the flat when they were delivered, and had taken them in. They were pressed like faces against glass; I ripped them free of the squeaky transparency and read the card: With love, G. Graham and I have no private names, references, or love-words. We use the standard vocabulary when necessary. A cold bruised smell came up from the flowers; it was the snowdrops, with their onion-like stems and leaves, their chilly greenness. He knows how crazy I am about them. And about the *muguet-du-bois* that we bought when we met for a week in the Black Forest in Europe last year. There is nothing wrong with a plain statement: with love. He happened to be in the florist's and so he sent me some flowers. It's not a thing he would do specially, unless it were on a birthday or something. It might have been because of Max; but good God, no, surely not, that would have been awful, he wouldn't have done it. We had made love the night before, but there was nothing special about that. One doesn't like to admit to habit, but the fact is that he doesn't have his mind on Court the next day, on Friday evenings, and I don't have to get up next morning to go to work.

While I was putting the flowers in water the phone rang again. "They're lovely—I've just come in this minute. The first snowdrops I've seen this year."

"How was he?"

"Oh, it was all right. He's a very sensible child, thank God."

I began to wish he would say come to lunch, but I wouldn't do anything about it because we make a point of not living in each other's pocket, and if I were to start it, I'd have to expect him to make the same sort of use of me at some time when it might not be convenient. You can't have it both ways. He was probably lunching at the house of the young advocate he'd been playing golf with; the wife is a lawyer, too, a nice girl—I enjoy their company and have a sort of open invitation from them, but before people like this, his colleagues, we don't like to give the impression of "going about everywhere together," we make it tacitly clear that we're not to be regarded as a "couple." There's no

point in a man like Graham flaunting the fact that he's got
a woman unless—what? I don't suppose you could say that
our affair wasn't serious; but all the same, it's not classified,
labelled.

Graham told me there was something about Max in the
early edition of the evening paper. "Do you want me to
read it?"

"No, just tell me."

But he cleared his throat as he does before he reads something aloud, or begins his plea in court. Unlike most lawyers he has a good voice. "It's not much. There's no mention of you, only his parents. The case is exhumed, of
course . . . and it says he was a named Communist—I
don't somehow remember . . . ?"

"Which he wasn't. He was never named. However."

"A diving team managed to bring up the car. There was
a suitcase full of documents and papers in the back, all so
damaged by water that it will not be possible to determine
their nature."

"That's good."

"Nothing else. —His father's career in Parliament."

"Oh yes. No mention of Bobo at all?"

"Fortunately not."

We might have been cool criminals discussing a successful
get-away.

I said, "It was a most perfect morning. Did you have a
good game?"

"Booker beat the pants off me. That's the second time
this week and I've told him it's once too often." He and his
golf partner had been opposing counsel in a case Graham
had lost.

I said, "I don't understand it. If I were you I should have

seen enough of him to last me for a bit." He laughed; I am always shocked by the way lawyers can attack each other with every sign of bitter ruthlessness over somebody's life—and then sit in brotherly bonhomie at the tea-break. "Nothing's more frightening than professionalism. Imagine, whether you get ten years or go free can depend on whether or not your counsel can out-talk the other man's, and there they are boozing together at the golf club. It terrifies me more than the idea of the judge. I like to think that when I go to a lawyer, he's as tied up in my affairs as I am myself."

We both laughed; on ground we'd gone over before.

"But you know that wouldn't do at all, he'd be giving very bad counsel if he were to be. You're too emotional."

I thought of how we'd just talked of Max's death. Honesty sounds callous; so that one is almost ashamed of it.

"Booker doesn't know we're going to appeal, anyway," he teased me drily. "I'll get my own back in court if not on the green. I'm going to do some work this afternoon, that is, if I don't sleep. I don't suppose I'll be able to resist a sleep. That chair you made me buy." In Denmark he ordered the beautiful leather furniture they make there, and we threw out the ugly stuff his wife must have thought suitable for a "gentleman's study." There's a chair you could sleep the whole night in, even make love in, not that he ever would. Yesterday after the servant had taken the coffee away, although the mood for love-making came as we sat in front of the fire, we went into his bedroom as usual. What nonsense it is to write of the "disembodied" voice on the telephone; all of Graham was there as he talked commonplaces. Last night he was held in my body a long time.

The call-box bleeped at his end and I said something again about the flowers, before we hung up. Once alone, I didn't feel the slightest inclination to go out, after all; I felt, on the contrary, a relief. I brought the water in the vase to the right level. I threw the paper and cellophane in the kitchen bin and put the food I'd bought into the refrigerator. I opened the creaking joints of my plastic and aluminium chair and sat on the balcony in the sun, smoking. Many of the demands one makes on other people are nothing but nervous habit, like reaching for a cigarette. That's something for me to remember, if I were ever to think of marrying again. I don't think I'll marry again. But I catch myself speaking of Max as my "first husband"; which sounds as if I expect to have another. Well, at thirty, one can't be too sure of what one may still do.

At eighteen I was quite sure, of course. I would be married and have a baby. This future had come out to meet me as expected, though perhaps sooner. Max might not have been the man according to specifications, but the situation, deep in my subconscious, matched the pattern I'd been given to go by. The concept of marriage as shelter remained with me, even if it were only to be shelter from parents and their ways. There, whatever the walls were made of, I should live a woman's life, which was?—a life lived among women like my mother, attached to a man like my father. But the trouble is that there are no more men like my father—in the sense that the sort of man my father is doesn't represent to me, in my world, what it did to my mother in hers. I was brought up to live among women, as middle-class women with their shopping and social and household concerns comfortably do, but I have to live among men. Most of what there was to learn from my family and background has turned out to be hopelessly obsolete, for me.

Graham and I have known each other since the trial. I was already divorced from Max, but there was no one else to do anything; that's how I met Graham, I was told he was the right man for the case. As it happened he couldn't take the brief, in the end it was given over to someone else, but he remained interested and afterwards, when Max was in prison, he helped me make various applications on Max's behalf. Graham didn't ask me any questions, he was like one of those doctors with whom you feel that he knows everything about you, simply from a professional reading of signs you don't even know you exhibit. He had a wife once; she was a girl he'd gone about with since they were school children, and she died of meningitis when she was younger than I am now. There are still traycloths in the house on which she embroidered her initials.

Graham defends many people on political charges and is one of a handful of advocates who ignore the possible consequences of getting a reputation for being willing to take such cases. I've got my job analysing stools for tapeworm and urine for bilharzia and blood for cholestrol (at the Institute for Medical Research). And so we keep our hands clean. So far as work is concerned, at least. Neither of us makes money out of cheap labour or performs a service confined to people of a particular colour. For myself, thank God shit and blood are all the same, no matter whom they come from.

In Europe last year, we enjoyed ourselves very much, and lived in the same room, the same bed, in easy intimacy. We each went our own way some of the time, but we'd planned the holiday together and we stayed together for the greater part. I don't think we once felt irritated with each other. Yet since we've been back we've lived again just as we used to, sometimes not sleeping together for two weeks, each taking up large tracts of life where the other has no claim. I didn't need him, sitting in the sun on my balcony.

A sexual connection. But there is more to it than that. A love affair? Less than that. I'm not suggesting it's a new form of relationship, of course, but rather that it's made up of the bits of old ones that don't work. It's decent enough; harms nobody, not even ourselves. I suppose Graham would marry me, if I wanted it. Perhaps he wants it; and then it would all change. If I wanted a man, here, at this time, in this country, could I find a better one? He doesn't act, that's true; but he doesn't give way, and that's not bad, in a deadlock. He lives white, but what's the point of the gesture of living any other way? He will survive his own convictions, he will do what he sets out to do, he will keep whatever promises he makes. When I talk with him about history or politics I am aware of the magnetic pull of his mind to the truth. One can't get at it, *but to have some idea where it is!* Yet when he's inside me—last night—there's the strangest thing. He's much better than someone my own age, he comes to me with a solid and majestic erection that will last as long as we choose. Sometimes he will be in me for an hour and I can put my hand on my belly and feel the blunt head, like a standard upheld, through my flesh. But while he fills me, while you'd think the last gap in me was closed forever, while we lie there silent I get the feeling that I am the one who has drawn him up into my flesh, I am the one who holds him there, that I am the one who has him, helpless. If I flex the muscles inside me it's as if I were throttling someone. He doesn't speak; the suffering of pleasure shuts his eyes, the lids are tender without his glasses. And even when he brings about the climax for us—afterwards I am still holding him as if strangled: warm, thick, dead, inside. That's how it is.

But I don't think of it often; and as I sat on my balcony in the midday sun that cannot possibly be called "winter," it simply took a place in my consciousness (I was growing drowsy from the dry warmth) with the pigeons toeing their way along the guttering, two children I couldn't see, but could hear shooting water pistols at each other, below my feet, and the men on the bit of grass above the pavement opposite. They were black men with their delivery bicycles, or in working overalls. They lay flung down upon the grass, the legends of firms across their backs. They were drinking beer out of the big red cartons, in the sun. We were all in the sun. There is a way of being with people that comes only by not knowing names. If you have no particular need of anyone, you find yourself belonging to a company you hadn't been admitted to before; I didn't need anybody because I had these people who, like myself, would get up and go away in a little while. Without any reason, I felt very much at home.

In spite of everything.

Their talk went on sporadically, in the cadences I know so well, even if I don't understand the words. It was the hour when all flat-dwellers were at lunch and only they had time to lie on the grass, time that had no label attached to it. After a while I went in and cut myself the crust of the loaf I'd bought and put some papery shop-ham on it and ate a banana in which there was winter—a hard centre and a felted taste. When I had food in my stomach I was overcome by weariness and lay down on the divan in the living room, where it was warm, under the rug from Bobo's bed.

A vision of seaweed swaying up from deep under water.

Not asleep but awake in the vision, as I opened my eyes in the room. At once close to the water where the heads surface in bunches of torn rubber ribbons sizzling with the oxygen of broken water, bedraggle in the wash from the rocks; and at the same time looking down from the cliff high where the road is, down on the depths tortoise-shell with sun and the rippling distortion of the great stems, brown thrashing tubes that sway down, down, out of the focus of lenses of water thick as bottle-ends, down, down.

The water rushed into Max's nostrils and filled his mouth as it opened for air. For the first time it came to me as it must have happened when he made it happen. The burning cold salt water rushing in everywhere and the last bubbles of life belching up from places where they had been caught—the car, under his shirt, in his lungs, filled with the final breath that he had taken before he went down. Down, down, to where the weeds must, at last, have their beginning. He took with him a suitcase of papers that could not be deciphered. So much sodden muck. He took them with him, and no one would ever know what they were—writings, tracts, plans, letters. He had succeeded in dying.

I was lying still in the room and my eyes were filled with tears. I wept not for Max's death but for the pain and terror of the physical facts of it. The flowers had stirred and opened while I slept and the warm room was full of scent. I lay quite still and felt myself alive, there in the room as their scent was.

Max's death is a postscript. A postscript can be something

trivial, scarcely pertinent, or it can be important and finally relevant.

I believe I know all there was to know about Max. To know all may be to forgive, but it is not to love. You can know too much for love.

When Max and I got married he left the university and took a job—many jobs. None of them lasted long; there were so many other things to do, at that time there were still things you could do whose immediacy appealed to us —discussion and study groups in the rooms of people like ourselves and in the black townships, open-air meetings, demonstrations. The Communist Party had been declared illegal and officially disbanded, but in the guise of other organizations the whole rainbow from politically conservative do-gooders to the radical Left wing could still show itself fairly openly. Above all, African nationalism was at a stage when it had gained confidence and prestige in the eyes of the world through the passive resistance campaigns, and at home seemed ready to recognize Africans of any colour who wanted to be free of the colour bar. In our little crowd, Solly, Dave, Lily, Fatima, Alec, Charles—Indian, African, Coloured, and white—Fatima gave Bobo his bottle, Dave laughed at Max's bad moods. The future was already there; it was a matter of having the courage to announce it. How much courage?—I don't think we had any idea.

Max's first job was abandoned because they wouldn't give him three days off to attend a Trades Union conference. Max had been reading politics as a major subject at the university, but there were great gaps in what he felt he ought to know; at the time he was concentrating on trying to give a small group of politically ambitious Africans some of the theoretical background in economics that they wanted. I forget what happened to the next job—oh yes, he got a typist to mimeograph some leaflet during office hours. And so it went on. The jobs came last in any consideration because they were of no importance. He took whatever he could get to do that would help to keep us going. He had no particular qualifications, anyway; he had been studying for an arts degree, which his parents had seen as a harmless alternative to commerce or accountancy, and which he had seen as freedom of mind. The nature of the degree didn't matter much to them; he'd been expected to join one of his father's companies on the accomplishment of it, that's all.

Max was supposed to be going on working for his degree, at night, but at night there was less time than during the day, since the study groups and meetings were all held after working hours, and friends came for sessions of talk that used to last half the night. I went back to work when Bobo was five months old, and we had a nanny, Daphne, a tough, pretty, real Johannesburg nanny who looked after Max, when he was at home, as well as the baby. Once she and I both suspected in the same month that we were pregnant, and, without my bothering Max or her telling her boyfriend, we managed to mend our situation by promptly taking some pills exacted from my doctor with a warning that they wouldn't work if we were.

I was possessed by the idea that Max must be able to go back to university full time and finish his course. We wouldn't live off the Van Den Sandts (we'd had to take help from them now and then—over Bobo's birth, for example). I wanted to find some work I could do at night, in addition to my daytime job. We examined the possibilities; I couldn't type. I said at last, "A cinema usherette. That's about all. I wonder what they get paid."

"Why not? With a Soutine pageboy's outfit and a torch."
I could see that the idea really pleased him. He began to
remark to people, as if I had already taken the job, "Liz's
going to be working in a cinema. Don't think you're seeing
things." I was working for a private firm of pathologists,
then, and instead of becoming an usherette I got the writing up of some research notes to do for one of the doctors.
It paid better than working in a cinema would have done,
and I was able to do it at home. But Max was often irritated by Dr. Farber's notes spread about in the cramped flat
where there was not enough room for his own books and
papers, and he seemed to lose interest in the purpose of my
extra job. To work as an usherette in a cinema was perhaps
the furthest point one could possibly get from any sort of
activity that Mrs. Van Den Sandt or beautiful Queenie
could have imagined themselves engaged in. I deprived
Max of an opportunity of reaching an ultimate in his distance from them, and of a gratification of his longing to come
close to other people in a bond of necessity. I was aware of
that longing, but I didn't always understand when I
failed to further its fulfilment.

Although Max had been a member of a Communist cell
at the university, he did not take a strictly Marxist line in
his attempts to give Africans some background for the evo-
lution of their own political thinking. And when the Communist Party began to function again, as an underground
organization, although he was approached to become active
under its discipline, he did not do so. He had been very
young and unimportant during his brief experience in the
Communist cell; maybe that had something to do with it
—he didn't see himself in that limited status, any more.

After the Defiance campaign, in which people of all sorts of political affiliation took part, he joined the new nonracial Liberal Party for a while, and then the Congress of Democrats. But the Africans themselves did not take the Liberal Party seriously; he saw himself set aside in a white group that Africans felt had the well-meaning presumption to speak for them. Even in the Congress of Democrats, a radical white organization (it provided a front for some important Communists) that did not confine itself to polite platform contacts at multiracial conferences, he was restless. The COD people worked directly with African political movements, but had come into being mainly because, while identifying themselves with the African struggle, they understood as a matter of tactics that no African movement seeking mass support can afford to have white members.

I hadn't joined the Liberal Party, but I worked in COD, not exactly with Max, but mostly on back-room stuff, printing propaganda for the African National Congress, and so on. You make curiously intense friendships when you work with the fear and excitement of police raids at your back. I believed in what I was doing and in the people I was doing it with. I certainly had enough courage to measure up to what was needed then—before Ninety Days—and I limited my activities only because of Bobo. Other people had children too, of course, and they put their political work first, but then if Max and I were both to have been arrested there would have been literally no one to look after Bobo but Daphne, since even the thought of his being taken over by the Van Den Sandts or my parents constituted, for me, real abandonment.

I'm mincing words. After all these years, because Max is

lying drowned. It's like putting on a hat for a funeral, the old shabby convention that one must lie about people because they're dead. The fact is, there was no one responsible for Bobo except myself. Max was unable to be aware of anyone's needs but his own. My mother once called this inability "horrible selfishness"; whereas it was the irreversible training of his background that she had admired so much, and that she saw him as a crazy deviate from. Driven to school and home again by the chauffeur every day, and then shut out of the rooms where the grownups were at their meetings and parties, at the Van Den Sandts he was ministered to like a prince in a tower. Even poverty didn't release him; and we were poor enough. He had the fanatic's few needs, and expected that they should be answered. He bought a pair of shoes or books or brandy on credit and was arrogantly angry when we were asked to pay; or assumed that I would deal with the shops. Max simply did not know what it was to live with others; he knew all the rest of us as he knew Raskolnikov and Emma Bovary, Dr. Copeland and Törless, shut up reading alone in his room on the farm. He would sit for hours analysing a man's troubles and attitudes with good insight and a compound of curiosity and sympathy, but he would not notice that the man was exhausted; nor would he remember that the man had mentioned that he had to catch a train home at a certain time. He used to take Bobo off down to Fordsburg to be handed about among the adoring young daughters of a multiple Indian household, and then, eager to follow up an acquaintance he'd perhaps made the night before, he'd go on to some yard or house and dump Bobo with a set of faces or a pair of arms—anybody's—the baby had never seen before. Once

Fatima phoned me to say that the mother of a cartage contractor in Noordgesig, the Coloured township, had rung her up to get my number, because Bobo was yelling and she didn't know what to offer him. Max had left with her son and Fatima's brother; left Bobo as he used to drop a bicycle or toy for the servants to pick up from the Van Den Sandts' lawn.

I tried to explain to Myra Roberts, a woman who seemed to me to have the only "saving grace" there is—a natural feeling of responsibility for strangers as for one's own family and friends—that COD couldn't count on both Max and me because of Bobo. She said, "Oh we feel we can count on you!"—and the emphasis made first my face burn and then hers. For a time I showed a certain coldness to her to make up for the disloyalty of that flush.

And yet Max would have done anything. That was somehow the trouble. When he was given a job he would always take it a stage beyond what he had been told was its intended limit. If (he was working on the news-sheet) he were asked to write a leader along certain lines, he would pursue the given conclusions further. He wrote well and would have liked to be editor of the news-sheet; if the executive could have felt assured that he would not use it to follow his own line and commit them where they did not choose to be committed, I think he'd have been made editor. In committee he sat charged with the desire to act—silent, shabby in his undergraduate nonconformist uniform of cracked veldskoen and blond beard, a nervous hand across his mouth. As they spoke—the experienced ones, who knew you must not risk bringing the banning of the organization nearer by one wasted word or step—his bright eyes paced them. And when they had finished he would seize upon the plan of action: "I'm seeing the trade union people tomorrow, anyway—I'll talk to them." "This's something that can only be done with the youth groupers. We'll have to get together with Tlulo and Mokgadi, Brian Dlalisa and that Kanyele fellow must be kept clear of—" A febrile impatience came from the sense that was always in him of being, in the end, whatever was done when working with white people like himself, outside the Locations and prisons and work gangs and overcrowded trains that held the heart of things.

But the others decided who should do what and they knew best who should approach whom. He would come home with the charge banked up glowing within him. The prescribed books on history, philosophy, and literary criticism lay about (I read them while he was busy at meetings); what on earth would he have done with a Bachelor of Arts degree, anyway? It was a dead end that would have served a rich man's son as a social token of attendance at a university. Perhaps he might have written something—he had passion and imagination; there were attempts, but he needed day-to-day involvement with others too much to be able to withhold himself in the inner concentration that I imagine a writer needs. He might have made a lawyer; but all the professions were part of the white club whose life membership ticket, his only birthright, he had torn up. He might have been a politician, even (it was in the family, after all), if political ambitions outside the maintenance of white power had been recognized. He might even have been a good revolutionary, if there had been a little more time, before all radical movements were banned, for him to acquire political discipline.

There are possibilities for me, but under what stone do they lie?

Max came home with a man called Spears Qwabe. He was a sodden, at-ease ex-schoolmaster who talked in a hoarse, soft voice. "The dangerous thing is we don't look to see what comes after the struggle, we don't think enough about what's there on the other side. You must know where you're going, man. You ask any of the chaps in town how he thinks we're going to live when we've settled with the whites. He's got a dreamy look in his eye thinking he'll get a car and a job with a desk, that's all. The same old set-up, only he's not going to sit in the Location or carry a pass. Even the political crowd don't know where they going, ideologically. ANC takes advice from the Commies, they willing to use their techniques of struggle, fine, okay, but apart from the few chaps who are Communists first and Africans second, who believes that ANC wants a society along orthodox Communist lines? They haven't got a social doctrine—all right, you can wave the Freedom Charter, but how far does it go . . . ? The same thing with PAC. Thinking just doesn't go beyond the struggle. And if it does—without making a noise about it, what d'you think it is? What's it amount to? Listen to them talk in their sleep and you'll hear they just want to take over the works—the whole white social and economic set-up, man, the job-lot. A black capitalist country with perhaps—I'll say maybe—the nationalization of the mines as a gesture. 'The mineral wealth beneath the soil, the Banks, and monopoly industry shall be transferred to the ownership of the people as a whole.' Nice poetry. But how they really going to work out an equitable distribution of what we've got? Does anybody talk sense about that? Does anybody bother to? And why should we have to take over any of the solutions of the East and West, cut-and-dried?"

"You will, largely, whether you like it or not, because you'll be taking over various institutions of the East and West, won't you, you're not going back to barter and cowrie currency—" Max wanted to encourage him, show him off.

"But wait—that's nothing—human institutions are adaptable, isn't it? What we need is to see ourselves as an industrialized people who can break out of the capitalist-Communist pattern set by the nineteenth century for an industrialized society, and make a new pattern. Break right out." He talked a long time that first day he came, but maybe I remember as what he said then also what I heard him say later, at other times. "We want a modern democratic state, yes? Tribalism will make it bloody difficult, even here, where tribalism's been just about finished off by the whites, anyway, although this government is playing it up again with Bantustans and so on. We must take the democratic elements of tribalism and incorporate them, use them, in a new doctrine of practical socialism. Socialism from Africa and for Africa. We don't need to go to the West or the East to learn about the evils of monopoly, man— land always belonged to the tribe, grazing belonged to the tribe. You don't have to teach us responsibility for the community welfare, we've always looked after each other and each other's children. All this must be brought into a new ethos of the nation, eh? The spirit of our socialism will come from inside, from us, the technical realization will come from outside."

Then Max began suddenly to rummage among our books

and piles of newspapers, and he handed him Nyerere's
book.

"Yes, yes—I know—but African socialism can't be the
work of one man. The doctrine of African socialism must
be made by different thinkers, all adding to it. We must
put it down, man. We've got political heroes, no thinkers.
Mbeki, yes, all right, perhaps. We'll have plenty political
martyrs, plenty more; no thinkers! We must put it down,
man!"

When Max was deeply interested, he had a way of standing before the person with whom he was in conversation,
literally closing in for an exchange. I remember how he
stood above the man in the dirty raincoat (even on the hot-
test day Spears held about him the late loneliness of a
rainy three in the morning) saying, "Yes . . . but the two
must run together, African socialism must be the philosophy of the struggle, it must be in at the struggle, *now*—if
it's going to mean anything—"

I liked Spears. He drank but although he couldn't always
manage his legs he never lost the use of his tongue. He had
a small coterie and they started calling themselves
"Umanyano Ngamandla," which meant something like
"Let's pull together," as a colloquial name for an African
socialist movement. Most of them were men who had
broken away from the African National Congress or Pan
African Congress. Max became their guru, or Spears became
his; it doesn't matter. COD ceased to exist in Max's consciousness, he didn't manage to return in decent order the
papers that belonged to work he had been doing. I know
that I went through our things to try and find them, but
months dragged by, we moved house, and I grew more and
more embarrassed at being asked for them. I had continued

to work with COD because I thought Max was wrong—it frightened me to see him simply *forget about* the people we had worked with there. But I began to see in the work COD did, if not in my friends who did it, limitations that were in the nature of such an organization and that had always been there: I needed Max to be right.

Spears was with us most of the time. He and Max were formulating his methodology of African socialism. Max saw it as a series of pamphlets that would become the hand-book, anyway, if not the bible, of the African revolution. We must put it down, man. The phrase was at once the purpose Spears lived by and the net of catchwords in which he tried to collect purpose when he was drinking; you could laugh at him when he repeated it drunk, go ahead and laugh at the infirmity of him: but it was like the name of a God, that does not alter in its omnipotence whether used as a curse or a blessing. *We must put it down, man.* I heard it all the time. It was the beat in his voice spacing the political clichés, grammatical constructions translated from Xhosa and literal translations from Afrikaans, of his strong-flavoured English.

And yet he did not see "putting it down" in quite the literal terms that Max did, that Max could not escape from. Max planned point by point, chapter by chapter (at one time he thought of writing the whole thing in the form of Platonic dialogues); but Spears' thinking erupted in a lava that, cooled to the process of note-taking, was difficult to break down into its component dissertation and analysis. Max and Spears talked late into the nights and every day Max wrote and recast from notes and memory. That was the time I came home from work and found Max yelling back at screaming Bobo. He had been trying to work all afternoon against the baby's noisy games and interruptions. Max's face was a child's mask of hysterical frustration: I took Bobo and walked in the streets with him, but there was nothing I could do for the face of Max.

For hours he stood planted, arguing in front of Spears, he couldn't stay put, in a chair. Spears was intense but quite without Max's tension; he could talk just as well sitting on the kitchen table while I fried sausages, or while Bobo climbed up and used his shoulders as a road for a toy car. He used to call me "Honey" and once or twice, when he was only a little drunk, he cornered me in the kitchen, but I told him I didn't like the smell of brandy, and he kneaded my hand regretfully and said, "Forget it, honey"; I think that most of his drive towards women had washed away in brandy, but the residue was an unspecified casual tenderness to which Bobo and I responded. And Max. Max most of all. There was Max standing urgently over him, protesting, arguing, pressing—it was not just the determination to *put it all down* that held Max there; he hovered irresistibly towards what could never be got down, what Spears didn't need to get down because it was his—an identity with millions like him, an abundance chartered by the deprivation of all that Max had had heaped upon himself. Some of the white people I know want the blacks' innocence; that innocence, even in corruption, of the status of victim; but not Max. And everyone knows those whites who want to be allowed to "love" the blacks out of guilt; and those who want to be allowed to "love" them as an aberration, a distinction. Max wasn't any of these. He wanted to come close; and in this country the people—with all the huddled warmth of the phrase—are black. Set aside with whites, even his own chosen kind, he was still left out, he experienced the isolation of his childhood become the isolation of his colour.

I don't know whether Max loved me. He wanted to make love with me, of course. And he wanted to please me—no, he wanted my approval, my admiration for whatever he did. These pass as definitions of love; I can think of others that are neither more nor less acceptable. This business of living for each other, that one hears about; it can just as well be living for the sight of one's self in the other's eyes. Something keeps two people together; that's as far as I'd go. "Love" was the name I was given for it, but I don't know that it always fits my experience. Someone has given Bobo the name, too; didn't he say, "I'm sorry I didn't love him"? What did he mean? Did he mean that he didn't need his father? Or that he didn't stop his father from dying?

I wanted to make love to Max, and I wanted to give him the approval he wanted, I wanted to please him. But it wasn't a matter of watching your husband rising a notch in the salary scale. What I wanted was for him *to do the right things so that I could love him*. Was that love?

Max was wonderful in bed because there was destruction in him. Passion of a kind; demonic sex; I've had it with others since. With every orgasm I used to come back with the thought: I could die like that. And of course that was exactly what it was, the annihilation, every time, of the silences and sulks, the disorder and frustration of the days. We moved four times in the first three years, each time in response to having reached another impossible situation— living in a one-room flat with a baby; working at home in a two-room flat with a baby; not being able to afford a larger flat on my salary; not being allowed to have Africans visit us in the building—and there was never time or money to make each place more than habitable. Everything had happened to us too soon; before we'd collected enough chairs to sit on the ones we had had begun to fall to bits.

It was Felicity Hare who tacked cotton cloth she had brought from Kenya round the packing-cases our stuff was moved in to converted outbuildings in someone's backyard. We used them as cupboards and tables. We had space there, and she lived with us for a time—a big, red-faced girl just down from Cambridge who wanted to "do something" in Africa. She had been handed on down the continent from territory to territory by introductions from friends of friends and always either in danger of being deported by a British colonial government when she became too friendly with African nationalists, or appealing to a British consulate for protection when African governments wanted her deported for becoming too friendly with members of their Opposition. She wore shorts and would follow you from room to room, talking, whatever you were doing, hitching herself on some ledge or table corner too small to support her, with her enormous, marbled legs doubled up in a great fleshy pedestal. Her conversation was confused and conspiratorial—"Actually, the woman in charge of the place wasn't American at all, she was a Dane, and the girls couldn't stick her. Couldn't understand what she was saying, d'y'know. That's another thing I didn't tell you—they came from about twenty different tribes and could scarcely understand English anyway. But there'd been some fiddle in the State Department—that's clear—and she wasn't the one who was supposed to be there, at all. The girls weren't learning a thing, but old Alongi Senga—" "Who's that?" "—Senga, Minister of Education, d'y'know, stupid old bastard, Matthew Ochinua says they say all he wants to do is inspect high schools so's he can pinch the boys' bottoms. Anyway, he'd had a row with the Field Service people—" Most of the stories ended with a shrug of the breasts and the big face gazing away, as if she had just discovered them, at her tiny hands with their little shields of bitten-down nail pressed into the plump pad of each finger: "So that was that . . ." "So I was off . . ."

She made herself useful doing some typing for Max and spent a lot of time getting people out of what she called "messes"—mostly the aftermath of parties she went to— taking home in her little borrowed car the corpses that piled up, staying the night with girls whose men had gone off with someone else. She patched the lining of Spears' raincoat and drove him on his complicated errands. There was the night I got up and found her dressed as if for a pic- nic, carrying a spray gun. "Going slogan-painting," she said. She went off with a tiny torch to wait to be picked up by whomever it was she was working with. I went back to bed and told Max. "A midnight feast for Sunnybunny! O wacko!" he said. The absurd play on her name was his in- vention; he and Spears treated her with the comradely mock-flirtatiousness that men show towards unattractive girls. I said, "Spears shouldn't tease her, it'll set her after him. She worships the two of you." "Why on earth not? Do Spears no harm, and she needs a man, our Sunbun."

She was always urging us to go to parties with her, but these were the parties where white liberals and black tarts and toughs went for what each could get out of the other. It surprised me that Max, once or twice, seemed willing to go. The work he and Spears were doing was going badly; Max was finding Spears evasive. Yet it became a sort of craze for the three of them—Max, Spears, and Sunbun—to appear at these parties as a weird trio. I dropped out because I couldn't last till three in the morning without drinking too much, and if I drank too much I couldn't work next day; if Max and Spears couldn't get on with their work, then, at least the parties provided a reason.

Often when I came home from the laboratory Max would be sitting waiting; punishing Spears with his waiting as a child believes he is punishing the grownup who is not even aware of being the object of resentment. When Bobo's voice rose in the kitchen, or shrieked in the bath, Max gave me one of his seizing looks. The calm of white coats and routine work, life apprehended as a neat smear under a microscope, came from me like the bar on the breath of a drunkard.

Felicity used to hover, importantly self-effacing. "I was desperate, d'y'know, he hasn't turned up all day. I made some excuse to go out and scout around but no one knew where he was." She spoke to me out of Max's earshot, as if he must not hear his condition discussed. Then Spears would arrive, and the casual tone of his excuses and apologies was not altered, whether Max was angry and sulky, or whether he suddenly was in a warm good mood and behaved as though Spears had not been expected until that particular moment. One night when this happened—the arrival of Spears at long last, and a quick rise in Max's mood—Max was moving about the room like a cork caught up off the sand by the tide, opening beer, offering cheese on the point of a knife, talking, putting papers together, and he pointed the knife at Felicity, saying in a cheerful impatient aside, "Come on, move that big arse, Sunbun, you know where you put the list I gave you—"

It was his way of talking to her and I was astonished, this

time, to see her cry. I suddenly understood that he had made love to her.

He stood there with the steel blade dulled with the grease of cheese, gesturing at her, and she rushed out of the room with all her flesh—buttocks, breasts—quaking; it was somehow specially moving, as if some poor peaceful browser had been stuck with a spear. I went after her and bumped into Daphne, holding a freshly-ironed dress that she must have tried to hand to her. I said quickly, "I'll take it."

"What she's got to cry for?" Daphne lifted her chin; she wanted me to know she knew, too.

Max said, "She bloody well wouldn't leave me alone. It started after a party and I was drunk anyway. She smothers you with her bloody great tits, you've got to fight your way out and that's the easiest way." It was true that one couldn't be jealous of Felicity. If she'd been a woman I had been jealous of it would have been different. But there was only one reason why Max made love to her. He knew it and I knew it. He needed approval and admiration so much that he was prepared to throw in a good fuck as payment. I could have forgiven his sleeping with a woman he wanted, but I couldn't forgive him the humiliation in her big shaking body when she ran out of the room. I used to think of it when we were making love. And I couldn't tell him because I myself couldn't give the approval and admiration.

Max shunned the Van Den Sandts' standards of success but in a way they triumphed in him, passing on, like a family nose or chin, the rage to succeed. He did not weigh in on their scale, but he retained the revengeful need *to be acknowledged*. It came from them: the desire to show somebody. What? The objects of his purpose were not demonstrable in the way that money and social prestige are. Why is it that these people always win, even if only by destruction?

Oh there were other women. When he went underground during the State of Emergency in 1960 he lived with Eve King while hidden in her house. And before that there was the thing with Roberta Weininger—beautiful Roberta, she's been under House Arrest for some time, now. These love affairs caused me pain, and in its context I had one or two affairs of my own. I suppose I thought of redressing the balance—some such expedient. But this again was the use of measures designed for a situation that had very little bearing on the realities of ours. If I'd only known, it didn't matter how many women Max had, it didn't make any difference. Whether or not he could really love a woman, me or any other woman, was not what was vital to him.

Spears went underground, too, but other members of "Umanyano Ngamandla" were detained and when they came out of prison the movement broke up; most of them, including Spears, rejoined the ANC, then banned and become an underground movement. The notes for the methodology of African socialism had been safe from the security raids on our back-yard cottage because I had bundled the papers into a laundry bag and kept it hidden in the laboratory, all the time. When Spears came to see me one day I told him they were intact; he smiled; the days of the work on the methodology belonged to another time. Decades, eras, centuries—they don't have much meaning, now, when the imposition of an emergency law or the fall of a bomb change life more profoundly in a day than one might reasonably expect to experience in a lifetime. Spears wasn't drinking. He didn't come often any more, and neither did William Xaba, another friend who always used to be in and out of the cottage. There was a move among politically active Africans to keep out of white houses, no matter whose they were, and to reject friendship and even intimacy with whites as part of white privilege. Max was in Cape Town then, for three months that stretched to six, working on a new radical journal whose editors were replaced as quickly as they were banned. Bobo and I went down for two weeks at Christmas and every day the three of us walked along the cliff road above the sea, where the polyps of seaweed reach up from far down in the water. "Look there. Look there," we urged Bobo, but his little boy's gaze would follow your finger as its object, and see no further than the end of it. I wonder if it was the papers of the African Socialist methodology that Max took down with him in the suitcase.

Between heliograph flashes of sun on water, undeciphered, there are still things that were said. "Christ, when you see how African women will live! They know how to wait. And to keep themselves and their children together. There's everything that matters to learn from them." Yes, he was right; I was an amateur in loneliness, in stoicism, in trust. "Maybe if you're ever going to achieve something, you'll have to do it quite alone." I said that once, knowing that already he was scornful of the journal he was working on, and (looking down at seaweed in the water like flowers imprisoned in a glass paperweight) seeing the end of this like the end of anything else he had begun. He didn't answer.

It was the last time we really lived together. He came back to Johannesburg and eventually we were divorced and he would disappear for months and turn up again. There was a rumour that he had slipped out of the country illegally and got in again. I didn't know whom he spent his time with, though I had heard through our old Indian friend Solly that he had associated himself for a while with people who wanted to organize a new underground white revolutionary group.

Then the telephone rang at eleven o'clock at night and he said, "Liz? That you Liz? When the papers come out— d'you get the morning paper? There may be something big. . . . Don't forget."

Nobody knows this. Nobody at all. I didn't even tell the lawyers. I have never told Graham. It's all that's left of Max and me; all there is still between us. That voice, wild and quiet, over the telephone.

The water covers everything, soon no bubbles rise.
There were possibilities, but under what stone? Under what stone?

Max's bomb, described in court as being made of a tin filled with a mixture of sulphur, saltpetre, and charcoal, was found before it exploded and he was arrested within twenty-four hours. Others were more or less successful and it all began again, and worse than it had ever been before; raids, arrests, detention without trial. The white people who were kind to their pets and servants were shocked at bombs and bloodshed, just as they had been shocked, in 1960, when the police fired on the men, women, and children outside the Sharpeville pass office. They can't stand the sight of blood; and again gave, to those who have no vote, the humane advice that the decent way to bring about change is by constitutional means. The liberal-minded whites whose protests, petitions, and outspokenness have achieved nothing remarked the inefficiency of the terrorists and the wasteful senselessness of their attempts. You cannot hope to unseat the great alabaster backside with a tin-pot bomb. Why risk your life? *The madness of the brave is the wisdom of life.* I didn't understand, till then. Madness, God, yes, it was; but why should the brave ones among us be forced to be mad?

Some fled the country, some were kept solitary in their cells and, refusing to speak, were kept on their feet under interrogation until they collapsed. Some did speak. Max was tried and sentenced to five years imprisonment but he was called as a State witness after serving fifteen months, and he spoke. He was beaten when he was first arrested, that we know, but what else he was confronted with later, what else they showed him in himself, we do not know— but he spoke. He spoke of Solly and Eve King and the man who was arrested with him, he spoke of William Xaba and other friends with whom we had lived and worked for years.

He is dead now. He didn't die for them—the people, but perhaps he did more than that. In his attempts to love he lost even his self-respect, in betrayal. He risked everything for them and lost everything. He gave his life in every way there is; and going down to the bed of the sea is the last.

⊓⊔⊓⊔
———
⊔⊓⊔⊓

*T*here's not much point in spending a long time with the old lady, my grandmother. As her memory's so bad, it doesn't make any difference whether you stay half an hour or two hours; so long as she sees you. She looks up from her indifference, which is the past, and in the daze of the present she finds a face—that's about all. I made a cup of coffee to wake myself up and then drove across the suburbs to the Home. It was intermission at the matinees; children thronged the cinema entrances pushing each other about and eating icecream in the sun. At a main intersection a down-at-heel white family hawked hanks of coloured spun sugar along the line of cars. People ran about on tennis courts I passed, and clustered on the bowling greens.

The empty red beer cartons were thick on every open space. If I were dumped back in it from eternity I should know at once that it was Saturday afternoon. It was in people's faces, the pleasure of the weekend, like the sweets clutched in children's hands.

The Home is an old house whose original iron-roofed colonial-Victorian has been knocked out and added on to. The entrance has steel and glass doors and tropical plants under concealed lighting, but on the first-floor landing there is a black wooden bear of the kind once designed to hold umbrellas in the crooks of his arms, and there are other ornately-carved survivals of the objects with which the new-rich, from Europe, of seventy years ago announced the change of status from successful gold prospector to mining magnate. There is even a stained glass window with the petals of cough-drop-coloured, *art nouveau* irises outlined in thick lead.

I've always felt that the place has a more human feel than any modern building designed as an institution, but when my grandmother first went there and was still able to care, she complained that it was ugly and old-fashioned. She loves plastics—artificial flowers, "simulated" silk, synthetic marble, fake leather. There was no sense of the day of the week, inside; the same warm air, faintly lit with methylated spirits, that comes back to me each visit as something I forget entirely in between. No seasons, either. Spring or winter, it feels the same. The corridors are covered with something that deadens footfalls and you pass the wide-open doors of wards where not all the patients are in bed, or old, either—it is a home for the chronically sick as well as the aged. I've got to know some of the shapes even before I recognize the faces—because of the particular position

which a malady will force someone to adopt in bed or chair.
Among the very small white-haired old ladies, the dying
diabetic, taking so long to die, was still there, humped on
her side, smoking. She has the reckless drinker's face that
diabetics sometimes have, and looks as if she had once been
good-looking—like a finished whore. But the distinguishing
marks of social caste are often distorted by illness; the home
is not cheap and it is unlikely that she belongs to anything
other than the respectable middle class. The monster with
the enormous belly was sitting on a chair with her legs
splayed out, like a dead frog swollen on a pond. I have
never known what is the matter with her.

Outside my grandmother's little room a bouquet stood in
a vase on the floor. Anemones, freesias, and snowdrops, exactly like mine.

I opened the door softly and stood a moment. She was sitting in a chair with a mouth drawn in lipstick on her face,
and her hair, which she had always kept short and tinted and
curled, pulled back into a skimpy knot. They dress her
every day and they had even put on her triple pearl choker
and huge button earrings. Her eyes flew open and in the
light that came from behind me I saw terror expand her
face and the red-drawn outline fall agape.

"Who is that!" she called out in horror.

"Don't be silly, now, it's Elizabeth, your grandchild—"
The nurse came across the room between us, but I said,
"Let her see me properly," and came over beside her where
the light from the window was on me, and kissed her, and
said, "Here I am, I didn't want to miss your birthday—"
She took the kiss and then drew back, still alarmed, and
looked at me, searching. "It's Elizabeth, isn't it, Elizabeth
my darling—" and though the Afrikaans nurse burst in

with assurances and cheerful laughter, took no notice. She motioned me to her and kissed me again. Then her hand went up to her mouth and pressed it and she said angrily, to the air, "Why haven't I got my teeth in, if Elizabeth is here. Where are my teeth?"

"Well, your gums was sore this morning, grannie, don't you remember? You didn't want to put it in. Wait, I'll bring it, I first want to put some of that stuff on—"

"What is she talking about? Give them to me!" The old lady clawed at the woman's hand and then, having got her teeth, concentrated carefully on the two plates before slowly deciding where uppers and lowers should go. The nurse was chattering; I suppose it is an enormous relief to have some company other than that of a senile old lady. "She always get a fright when somebody come to the door. I don't know why she's so scared, you know . . . since this last lot of angina attacks. I don't know what it is, she seem to think someone's going to come and get her. . . . I always say," and now she turned to my grandmother, playful, soothing, "nobody going to hurt you, grannie, nobody can do you any harm here, isn't it? I *tell* her."

A slight, distracted dent between the bald eyebrows showed that the old lady was aware of some habitually bothersome background noise. With her big, regular false teeth in her mouth she speaks in a high, controlled voice behind them, to avoid their distortion, but even then there is thickness and sibilance, as though she were speaking through a medium. "And the husband? With you, or away again at the moment? And Bobo? How is that sweet boy?"

She forgets that I was divorced from Max, and if I were to tell her he is dead, she would forget that, too. In her room with the signed photographs of famous artists on the walls (she has her own things around her) it always seems that nothing has happened. Or that everything has already happened. I sat under Jascha Heifetz facing Noel Coward and the framed menu of the lunch where she had met him in 1928, and told her that I had seen Bobo in the morning; he wished her a happy birthday.

"It's my birthday?" she said. And repeated it at intervals so that I had to explain again and again. "How old is it this time?"

"Eighty-seven." I wasn't sure.

She pulled a little-girl face, relic of the sham simplicity of her sophistication. "Horrible. Too long."

"It's my birthday? I didn't know . . . I don't know anything."

I patted her hand, in which the pulse throbbed everywhere. They keep her nails painted red, as she used to, but the effect, like the pearls round her neck, is recognizable not as a familiar adornment but as something done to her.

I said, "Have you seen the flowers I sent?" and the nurse chipped in, "She won't have it in the room. I arrange it nicely but she don't want it near her."

"Why? —But why don't you want your flowers in here?" The old lady's face went empty.

"Do they smell too strong? Don't you like the scent? I'm afraid it's not the time of year for roses." She used to talk about how much she loved roses—perhaps because she had very little interest in natural things, and roses were a safe choice.

"Yes, I think it's the smell she find too strong. It must be.

I brought it in and show it to her, but she won't have it!"

My grandmother looked from the nurse to me. "Who is that?" she asked me, pointing at her. Her face drew together in accusation. The nurse began to bustle, smiling, cajoling, "*Ag*, grannie, it's me, Sister Grobler—" but my grandmother dismissed the explanation with an impatient flicker of the facial muscles and said to me, "Who is she? What is she doing here?"

I told her, and she seemed satisfied and then said, "Is she good to me?"

I said yes, yes of course she was good to her. The nurse was cataloguing in a sing-song lullaby voice, "I make your bed . . . I bath you . . . I make your hair nice . . . I make you your cocoa . . ." but for my grandmother, again, she did not exist. The hands with the sunken hollows between the knuckles twitched now and then; they have never done any work, and my grandmother used to lavish pride and creams on them. She has lived on dividends all her life (her father was an engineer associated with Rhodes and Beit) but—my mother says—she won't leave any behind her, the expenses of her senility are eating up the last of her capital. My grandmother's capital has been a source of bitterness at home as long as I can remember; my mother's father left no specific provision for his children, and her marriage to a penniless young man happened to coincide with my grandmother's own second marriage to a man not much older than her daughter's on whom she spent the greater part of this capital and certainly all that she might have been expected to provide for the advancement of her daughter. It would have been useful if she could have left some money to Bobo, but there it is. Oddly, she never shared my parents' attitude to the way Max and I lived, and, vague about the nature of Max's shortcomings as a husband and provider as related by my mother, seemed to assume that he was merely rather a high-spirited and headstrong boy, some sort of charming adventurer (she had known a few) translated into present-day terms; some fashion she hadn't caught up with yet.

My mother and father were extremely gratified to have me "marry into" the Van Den Sandts, although I'd spoiled the dignity of the alliance somewhat by being pregnant before the wedding. Yet even if people in our small town were able to say meaningfully that he'd had to marry me, the son of a wealthy M.P. was a son-in-law most of them would have liked for a daughter of their own. My parents will be equally gratified, now, to know that he is dead. Is that too hard a thing to say? The son of a wealthy M.P.— that was what they expected of Max, and they didn't get it. But didn't I, in my way, expect something of him that he wasn't? The summer I was seventeen, the summer I met Max, I was helping out, for Christmas, in my father's shop. The fancy goods counter, with painted "coasters" for glasses, cheap cuckoo clocks and watches, maroon vases with gilt fluted tops, Japanese bridge pencils with tassels, German cork-screws with dogs' heads, china figurines of ballet dancers. Shop girls came in and bought these things with the money that they earned in other shops, selling similar stuff. Black men lingered a long time over the choice of a watch that, paid for out of notes folded small for saving, would be back within a week, I knew, because those watches didn't work properly. I had seen nothing of the product of human skills except what was before me in my father's drapery shop–cum–department store, but I knew there must be things more worth having than these, and an object in life less shameful than palming them off on people who knew nothing better to desire. The shoddy was my sickening secret. And then I found that Max knew all about it; that the house he lived in, and what went on there, his surroundings, though richer and less obviously unattractive, were part of it, too, and that this quality of life was apparently what our fathers and grandfathers had fought two wars abroad and killed black men in "native" wars of conquest here at home, to secure for us. Truth and beauty —good God, that's what I thought he would find, that's what I expected of Max.

When my grandmother dies, Bobo will get her father's gold hunter and chain, that Beit gave him.

After the first five minutes with her, as usual, I didn't know what to say. Searching the deep vacancy of her face for what lies lost there, I drew up from the trance of age her old pleasure in streets and cities, and described an imaginary shopping trip I had taken in the morning. "I was looking for something for the evening—you know, soon the weather will be getting warmer, and I want something light, but with sleeves. . . ."

Slowly her attention surfaced and steadied. "What are they wearing this year? Will it be black?"

"Well, no. I thought I'd like white, as a matter of fact, not *dead* white . . ."

She was leaning forward confidentially: "Hard on the face," she said.

"Yes . . . But off-white, something soft and simple."

"Always at the cleaners, my darling. You can only wear it once. And did you see what you wanted?"

"I went from shop to shop . . . it was so crowded. One

shouldn't try to buy clothes on a Saturday. I had coffee at Vola's—you remember, you used to like the coffee there. And the day when you took Bobo for lunch and he went and stole the rolls off the next table . . . ?"

Very slowly the smile began, cracking the line of the mouth, lop-sided and then coming through the whole deserted face, inhabiting it once more. We giggled together.

" 'Grannie, help yourself.' 'Grannie, help yourself.' " The precise memory was turned up; she was quoting Bobo.

The nurse broke in, "You see? Look how lively she is! —You can remember everything so nice when you want to! You see, when your granddaughter comes you can *really* talk nice . . . it's just you get lazy here with me. . . ." Her red plump arms had pointed elbows the shape of peach pips as she waved them about.

The old lady's face drained of meaning. I chatted on but she gave me only a slow blinking glance, half-puzzled, half-indulgent. I was talking but there was a dignity, final, bed-rock, in her ignoring me; it was true that I was saying nothing.

She said suddenly, "What happened?"

There is nothing to say.

She asks now only the questions that are never answered. I can't tell her, you are going to die, that's all. She's had all the things that have been devised to soften life but there doesn't seem to have been anything done to make death more bearable.

"If I can't go out any more, what shall I do, then?"

"Perhaps you could go out. Perhaps I could take you and Sister Grobler to a film one afternoon."

"But will I understand? —What shall I do, then?"

I said to her with a meaningless reassuring smile, "Stay here, quietly . . ."

"But tell me, what happened?"

I said, "Nothing has happened. There's nothing wrong. It's just old age, quite natural, quite normal. You are eighty-six—seven—it's a great age."

Soon the hour I'd stipulated to myself was up and I said good-bye to her with the usual bright smiles and promises that I should see her again next week (if I don't go for a month she won't know the difference). She was repeating, "It's old age, old age, great age, you are teaching me—"

As I got out of the door of the Home my own step came back to me after the silence of the corridors, quick, clipped, heel-and-toe on the paving, exhilarating and . . . slightly cruel. On the walls of the viaduct I have to drive under on my way home I noticed again the arrow-and-spear sign that has been there for a long time, now, the red paint still not entirely faded, and an unfinished message: TORTURE THE END. Perhaps it is one that Sunbun wrote. Whoever it was, was interrupted. There was one of those sunsets beginning —the kind we've been having for months. Buildings and telephone poles were punched black against a water-colour sky into which fresh colour kept washing and spreading, higher and higher. We've never seen so high before; every day the colours go up and up to a hectic lilac, and from that, at last, comes the night. People carry their drinks outside not so much to look at the light, as to be in it. It's everywhere, surrounding faces and hair as it does the trees. It comes from a volcanic eruption on the other side of the world, from particles of dust that have risen to the upper atmosphere. Some people think it's from atomic tests; but it's said that, in Africa, we are safe from atomic fall-out from the Northern Hemisphere because of the doldrums, an area where the elements lie becalmed and can carry no pollution.

*G*raham was here. He came at six. I was slicing onions for the pork fillets and opened the door with the knife in my wet hand. I'd said this morning I was going out for dinner—but there was nothing to be done about it. My smelly hands were there held stiffly away from me. He had my newspaper that he'd picked up from the doormat, and while I saw from the faintest possible movement at the corners of his long mouth that he understood, he said, "So the Americans have brought it off, too. They've had a man walking in space—look at this—" Not able to touch the paper, I twisted my neck to see the front-page pictures of a dim foetal creature attached by a sort of umbilical cord to a dim vehicle. "I wish they wouldn't try to print newspaper pictures in colour. You'd see much better if it were in plain black and white. It looks like something from one of Bobo's comics."

He wandered into the living room, opening up the paper while I closed the kitchen door and then disappeared into the bathroom to wash my hands. He was reading aloud the subheadings and bits of the long report: "He was several times ordered to return to the space craft, but he seemed to be enjoying himself out there. . . . 'Quit horsing around' came the terse order. . . . No More Cookies . . . crumbs from Southern-style corn muffins posed a minor problem. . . ." I laughed and called out comments while scrubbing my fingernails. The smell didn't come off. I came back into the living room rubbing lotion into my hands and he was sitting in his usual chair; it was not necessary, or possible, any more, to make an excuse or explanation. Only I could still smell the onion, if my hands moved close to my face.

He said, "I walked down. D'you know that it doesn't take more than twenty-five minutes?"

"Well, no, I don't suppose it would. It's downhill most of the way. But going back! D'you remember one day at Easter when my car wouldn't start and I walked home from your house?"

"When was that? But why didn't I drive you?"

"You'd lent your car to that fellow from the World Council of Jurists, don't you remember?"

"Oh, Patten, yes. Well, I'll have a drink and start the long trek before it gets too dark."

"No, I can run you back. There's plenty of time for me to dress." Now that I couldn't explain, it was so easy to maintain a lie.

He smiled and said casually, "Oh, fine," and got up to get the whisky bottle out of the cupboard. He supplies the whisky; I can't afford to. I went to shut the balcony doors because it was getting chilly. The super-sunset was still framed there, a romaticized picture that made the room look drab. He said, "It's magnificent."

"I'm getting used to them."

He went on looking, so that I couldn't close the doors, and waited for him to have had enough, like a patient attendant at a museum. "I'd like a few cows and lovers floating above Fredagold Heights, though," he said. He has a Chagall drawing in his bedroom; curious; the way some women have a Marie Laurencin print in theirs. Why not in the living room? There is some private vision, version of life to which the public one doesn't correspond. Or into which the public is not allowed. And yet he had never been interested in Chagall until a rich client gave him the drawing. Then he hung it in the bedroom.

"Suppose it is fall-out," I said.

"Well?" He is sometimes a little patronizing towards me, though not offensively.

"Then it's not beautiful, is it."

"There's nothing moral about beauty." He smiled; we were having what he calls an "undergraduate chat."

"Truth is *not* beauty."

"Apparently not."

I closed the doors but I couldn't very well pull the curtains; he sat with his drink in his hand, the chair hitched round to face the view.

I hardly notice these sunsets any more, but his attention attracted mine as one's attention is attracted by someone's absorption in a piece of music one has heard too often and ceased to hear. I said, gazing because he was gazing, following the colour, "If it is fall-out there's something horrible about it looking like that."

"How does it look to you?"

I couldn't see any floating lovers or fiddles or cows, out there. "Like the background to a huge Victorian landscape. Something with a quotation underneath with lots of references to the Soul and God's Glory and the Infinite. Something that ought to have a scrolled gilt frame weighing twenty pounds. It's what my grandmother would have been taught was beautiful, as a child. You know, that style. What's it got to do with us. And with bombs."

"It's a bit picture-postcard, but still."

"All the dawns and sunsets in all the albums rolled into one. The apotheosis of picture-postcard. Just imagine a colour photograph of that, exhibited in a hundred years' time. Things are not like that with us at all."

The dark was coming now, graining the texture of the lilac space. A sharp star came through like a splinter of glass. Usually when I say something that doesn't particularly engage his mind, but that he thinks sensible, he will say, "You have a point there." It doesn't exactly irritate me; it is one of the gauges in which I read what he thinks of me. When people know each other as well as he and I do this is what is really taking place all the time, no matter what they are talking about. Never mind whether they're discussing politics, or gossiping about friends, or planning a holiday —the important thing is the constant shifting and maintaining of balance, the endless replaying of the roles each has secretly chosen the other to present, and which the other secretly contrives to appear to fulfil by nature. Even though I know I'm a damned intelligent woman—by far

the most intelligent female he's ever had any sort of deal-
ings with—and that a relationship with a woman of my
kind implies the acceptance not only of intellectual equal-
ity but also coeval common-sense (none of the patronizing
affection towards precocious feminine cleverness)—in spite
of this, even when I'm holding up my end in discussion a
shade better than he is, there's a sort of backwards glance, in
me, at my performance before him. And this corresponds to
a hidden expectation from him that he will be intrigued by
the quality of a female mind—that mind whose quality is
accepted rationally as taken for granted. In Europe last
year, arguing about paintings and buildings we saw together, in discussions of various kinds at friends' dinner
tables, in his house or my flat, talking politics as we do most
of the time—underneath, he coaxes me, and I show off to
him, I coax him and he performs for me.

While we were talking I was aware, as if standing aside
from us both, that this other dialogue of ours was sooth-
ingly being taken up. Our speaking voices went on, a bit
awkwardly, but, like the changing light in the *Son et
Lumière* performances we saw in France, illuminating, independent of the narration, the real scene of events as it
moved from walls to portal, to courtyard and window, the
light and shadow of the real happening between us was
going on as usual, in silence.

Then instead of saying, "You have a point there,"
Graham said, "How would you say things are with us?"

For a second I took it as going straight to all that we
competently avoided, a question about him and me, the lie
he had caught me out with on my hands—and I could feel
this given away, in my face.

I did not know what to say.

But it was a quiet, impersonal demand, the tone of the judge exercising the prerogative of judicial ignorance, not the partisan one of the advocate cross-examining. There was what I can only describe as a power failure between us; the voices went on but the real performance had stopped in darkness.

I said, "Well, I'd find it difficult to define—I mean, how would you describe—what could one say this is the age *of?* Not in terms of technical achievement, that's too easy, and it's not enough about us—about people—is it?"

"Today, for instance." He was serious, tentative, sympathetic.

Yes, this day. This morning I was driving through the veld and it was exactly the veld, the sun, the winter morning of nine years old, for me; for Max. The morning in which our lives were a distant hum in the future, like the planes a distant hum in the sky (there was a big air force training camp, near my home, during the war). Grow big, have a job, be married, pray to the blond Christ in the white people's church, give the nanny your old clothes. This same morning and our lives were here and Max had been in prison and was dead and I was not a widow. What happened? That's what she asked, the old lady, my grandmother. And while I was driving through the veld to see Bobo (Max heard the ducks quacking a conversation he never understood) a man was walking about in space. I said, "Graham, what on earth do you think they'll call it in history?" and he said, "I've just read a book that refers to ours as the late bourgeois world. How does that appeal to you?"

I laughed. It went over my skin like wind over water; that feeling you get from a certain combination of words, sometimes. "It's got a nice dying fall. But that's a political definition, they're no good."

"Yes, but the writer—he's an East German—uses it as a wider one—it covers the arts, religious beliefs, technology, scientific discoveries, love-making, everything—"

"But excluding the Communist world, then."

"Well no, not really"—he loves to give me a concise explanation—"it exists in relation to the early Communist world—shall we call it. Defining one, you assume the existence of the other. So both are part of a total historical phenomenon."

I poured him another drink because I wanted him to go, and although he wanted to go, he accepted it. "Did you work all afternoon? Or did you really sleep?"

But I knew that he had worked; he gave the admission of a dry, dazed half-smile, something that came from the room where he'd been shut up among documents, as a monk, who during his novitiate still makes some sorties into the life outside, is claimed by the silence of the cell that has never really relinquished him. Even the Friday night love-making had not made Graham sleepy in the afternoon; in that room of his, he wrote and intoned into the dictaphone, alone with his own voice. I've heard it sometimes from outside the door; like someone sending up prayer.

I mentioned I'd noticed that the arrow-and-spear sign was still on the walls of the viaduct near the Home.

"I'm not surprised. I think there are a few new ones round the town, too. Somebody's brave. Or foolhardy." He told me last week that a young white girl got eighteen months for painting the same symbol; but of course in the

Cape black men and women are getting three years for offences like giving ten bob's worth of petrol for a car driven by an African National Congress member.

"D'you think it's all right, using that spear thing? I mean, when you think who it was who had the original idea." It came out in a political trial not long ago that this particular symbol of resistance was the invention of a police *agent provocateur* and spy. I'd have thought they'd want to find another symbol.

He laughed. "I don't suppose the motives of the inventor've much to do with it. After all, look at advertising agencies—do you think the people who coin the selling catchword believe in what they're doing?"

"—Yes, I suppose so. But it's queer. A queer situation. I mean one could never think it would be like that."

We were silent for a moment; he was, so to speak, considerately bare-headed in these pauses in which the thought of Max was present. There was nothing to say about Max, but now and then, like the silent thin spread of spent water coming up to touch your feet on a dark beach at night, his death or his life came in, and a commonplace remark turned up reference to him. Graham asked, "The flowers arrive for your grandmother all right?" I told him how they were kept outside the door; and how she had cried out when she saw a figure in the doorway.

"It's natural to be afraid of death." Just as if he were advising a dose of syrup of figs for Bobo (one of the fatherly gestures he sometimes boldly makes). "Maybe. But she's never had to put up with what's natural. Neither grey hairs nor cold weather. It's true—until two or three years ago, when she became senile, she hadn't lived through a winter in fifteen years—she flew from winter in England to the summer here, and from winter here to summer in England. But for this, now, nothing helps."

"Like the common cold," he said, standing up suddenly and looking down at me; almost amusedly, almost bored, accusingly. So he dismisses a conversation, or makes a decision. "Can you take me now?" But he doesn't understand. Since you have to die you ought to be provided with a perfectly ordinary sense of having had your fill. A mechanism like that which controls other appetites. You ought to know when you've had enough—like the feeling at the end of a meal. As simple and ordinary as that.

I drove him home. His name is on the beautifully polished bronze plate on the gateway and a wrought-iron lantern is turned on by the servants at dusk every day above the teak front door. When he got out of the car I asked him to supper tomorrow. There was no difficulty about the lie; it didn't seem to matter at all, everything was slack and somehow absent-minded, between us. As soon as I'd dropped him, I drove home like a bat out of hell, feeling pleasurably skilful round corners, as I find I do when I've had just one sharp drink on an empty stomach. I had to get on and finish with the onions and have a bath, before half past seven.

I'd said about half past seven, but I could safely count on eight o'clock, so there was plenty of time.

I was expecting Luke Fokase. He phoned the laboratory on Thursday. "Look, how are things, man? I'm around. If I should drop in on Saturday, is that all right with you? I'm just around for a short time but I think I'll still make it."

We don't use names over the telephone. I said, "Come and eat with me in the evening."

"Good, good. I'll drop by."

"About half past seven."

I don't know why I asked him again. I rather wish he'd leave me off his visiting list, leave me alone. But I miss their black faces. I forget about the shambles of the back-yard house, the disappointments and the misunderstandings, and there are only the good times, when William Xaba and the others sat around all day Sunday under the apricot tree, and Spears came and talked to me while I cooked for us all. It comes back to me like a taste I haven't come across since, and everything in my present life is momentarily automatous, as if I've woken up in a strange place. And yet I know that it was all no good, like every other luxury, friendship for its own sake is something only whites can afford. I ought to stick to my microscope and my lawyer and consider myself lucky I hadn't the guts to risk ending up the way Max did.

Luke isn't one of the old crowd, but his pal, Reba, knew Max, and that is how they both happened to come to me. They live in Basutoland, though of course they really belong here but were somehow able to prove their right to Basuto citizenship and papers from the British administration there. Reba has some building and cartage contracting business and he sends his old truck quite freely up and down between Maseru and Johannesburg with loads of second-hand building material. Apparently it provides an unscheduled bus service for politicals on the run, and even transports people in the other direction, taking them up to the Bechuanaland border. One night about fifteen months ago Reba arrived at my flat in the middle of the night; the truck had broken down with two chaps on board who had arranged to be escorted over the border that night, and he didn't have enough money to pay for the repairs. I'd only met him once before, with Max, and I wasn't quite sure if I really knew who he was, but I lent him what I had—eight pounds. I was afraid to—he could easily have been a police trap—but I was even more afraid not to; how could someone like me risk losing two Africans their chance to get away?

He had with him that night a plump young man with a really black, smooth face—almost West African—and enormous almond eyes that were set in their wide-spaced openings in the black skin like the painted eyes of smiling Etruscan figures. That was Luke. Reba is a little, vaseline-coloured man whose head is jammed back between his shoulders like a hunchback's and who holds his big jaw full of teeth open in an attentive, silent laugh, while you're speaking, as a hippopotamus keeps his ajar for the birds to pick his teeth. They were an immensely charming pair who gave the impression of being deeply untrustworthy. I didn't expect to see the money again, but a registered envelope arrived with the notes and a letter of thanks idiotically signed "yours in the Struggle, Reba Shipise." Since then, Luke turns up from time to time; he says, alternately, apparently not remembering from one visit to the next what explanation he gave last time—that Reba is too busy with his business or that Johannesburg has become "too hot" for him. What does it matter? It's none of my business, anyway. They're both PAC men, too; and Max and I, like most white Leftists and liberals, always supported ANC people because they are not "racialist" and don't count us out, but the Government doesn't make any fine distinction between those who are said to want to push the white man into the sea and those who merely want their majority vote—both kinds can rot in prison together. What does the fact that they are PAC rather than ANC matter, either? All the old niggling scruples of the days before black political parties were banned seem quite to have missed the point, now.

It's not often that I cook a proper meal, unless Bobo's home on holiday; Graham can afford to buy our dinner in a restaurant, or we can eat at his house, where there's a cook—it's not worth the trouble for me to have to start work in the kitchen when I come home from the laboratory. So that the mere fact of cooking something that requires more skill and organization of tasks than frying an egg makes quite an occasion for me—it doesn't matter whom it's for. Anyway, Luke Fokase is always hungry. That first night he came with Reba he sat down and ate cold friga-delles I happened to have in the refrigerator. Pork fillets cooked buried in lots of thinly-sliced onion are a bother to do, but I rather enjoyed getting everything prepared right up to the stage when all I should have to do was set it cook-ing, just before we wanted to eat. I opened a bottle of Spanish red wine that Graham had left in case we should happen to eat something worthy of it here, sometime—wine is very important to Graham, I notice that a good dinner and good wine and then love-making go together, with him, he doesn't really enjoy the last without the first. I took a glass into the bathroom, and drank it in the bath. It looked lovely, the dark pansy-red against the tiles. I had the news-paper with me and I read the whole report from which Graham had read out bits about the space flight. There was nothing in the paper about Max; it had already been dropped from this, the late final edition.

Even then I was dressed and ready long before Luke came, and did not know what to do with myself. There are so many things that ought to be done when I have the time, but an awkward little wedge of time like this is not much use. Whatever I began, I should not finish. I can never go back to a half-written letter; the tone, when you take it up again, doesn't match.

And yet to put on a record and pour myself another glass of wine and sit—something that sounds delightful—made me feel as if I were on stage before an empty auditorium. I fetched the book I was reading in bed in the morning. Since I stopped half-way down the page at which a dry cleaner's slip marked my place, there was Max's death; it seemed to me a different book, I can't explain—it sounded quite differently there in that inner chamber where one hears a writer's voice behind the common currency of words. The voice went on and on but ran into itself as an echo throws one wave of sound back and forth on top of another. I read the words and sentences, but my mind twitched to the single electrical impulse—the death of Max. As soon as I gave up the attempt to read, it was all right again. I wasn't even thinking about him. Through the walls there was the muffled clatter of dinner-time in the flats on either side of mine, and the bark of someone's radio at full volume. Car doors slammed and the clear winter air juggled voices. Our lights blazed at Fredagold Heights and theirs blazed back. I saw the tube of glue lying in the ashtray (I'd had it out to stick down the sole of my shoe a few days ago) and remembered that I had never got round to mending the head of the baboon mascot I brought back for Bobo from Livingstone, on the way home from Europe last year. It came broken out of my overnight bag; and after showing it to him I'd put it away among my cosmetics, telling him I'd stick the snout on. I went to the bedroom and found it, at the back of the drawer; one of the red lucky-bean eyes had come out, too, but I found that as well, in the fluff and spilt powder. The thing is made of some unidentifiable fur (meerkat? rat?), well-observed, with an obscenely arched tail, and a close-set, human expression about the bean eyes in a face carved out of a bit of soft wood. I glued both broken surfaces very carefully and then pressed them together accurately. I scraped off with my fingernail the hairline of glue squeezed out along the break and then held snout and head tightly while the fusion set; you wouldn't be able to tell that it was mended. I began to think about how one day I would buy albums and begin to stick in the photographs of Bobo as a baby that are lying in an old hatbox on the top of the bathroom cupboard. Most of the others—him as a little boy—went along with our personal papers and cuttings in security raids on the old cottage, and I've never been able to get them back. Sticking Bobo's pictures into an album and recording the dates on and places where they were taken suddenly seemed enthusiastically possible, just as if the kind of life in which one does this sort of thing would fly into place around us with the act. My stomach was rumbling hunger, and with fingers tacky with glue, I had just poured myself another glass of wine when there was a soft, two-four beat rapping at the door; Luke doesn't ring bells.

He doesn't worry about being seen, either. I know that he comes straight up through the front entrance of the building, so that the watchman, who sits on his box on the lookout for people sneaking up to the servants' rooms on the roof by way of the back stairs, won't bother him, and if he met the caretaker—somehow he doesn't—he'd spin her a plausible, breezy yarn to account for his presence, and get away with it, too. There are some Africans who can do these things; others can't move a step without getting entangled in the taboos all round their feet. I learnt that while Max was working with them. When he—Luke—stood in the doorway I realized that he is not present to me in any way when I don't hear or see him. He exists only when his voice is on the other end of the telephone or when he stands there like this, a large, grinning young man, filling his clothes. And yet I felt happy to see him. He is immensely *there*—one of those people whose clothes move audibly, cloth on cloth, with the movement of muscle, whose breathing is something one is as comfortably aware of as a cat's purr in the room, and whose body-warmth leaves fingerprints on his glass. He came in heavily and I put down the catch on the Yale. "Good—great—good to see you . . ." He put his hands at once on the top of my arms and let them slide down towards the elbows, squeezing me gently. We stood there a moment, grinning, flirting. "And you, I'd forgotten what you look like . . ." "Hey, what's this, what's here—have I been away *so* long?" It was a light hair he had found and pulled out, on top of my head. "Nonsense, it's the newest thing. They do it at the hairdresser, it's called streaking . . ." It was a game; he gave me a little appraising lift, with the heel of the hand, on the outer sides of my breasts, as one says, "There!" and we went into the living room.

He was talking, wandering round the room, looking, touching here and there, to establish intimacy at once, to show that he was at home; or reading the signs—who had been there, what sort of claims had left their mark, what was the state of my life expressed there. I could see that—from the point of view of information—he missed the flowers that, to me, walking into a room like this, would have had something to say immediately. But, fairly familiar though he may be with the normal trappings of white people's homes, he's not familiar enough to notice the significant difference between a bunch of flowers that a woman like me might have bought on a street-corner and an expensive bouquet from a florist. "I came down on Tuesday—no, it was *very* late we left, Wednesday, early on Wednesday morning, really. Something wrong with the car—"

"—Naturally." I held up the brandy bottle in one hand, the open wine bottle in the other.

"Oh anything. Brandy. Well, the fan-belt was gone and the chappie I was with—"

"Aren't you here with the truck? How's old Reba?"

"Okay; he just sticks at home these days and leaves me to do the moving around. He's had a lot of trouble with his wife—I don't know, she bumps into things without realizing. Something with the balance. The doctor can't find out. As a matter of fact, Reba said to ask you."

"Well, I'm not a doctor . . . it sounds like middle ear."

"Yes, that's right, that's what the doctor says, but she's not keen . . ." I laughed—"But she can't pick and choose —there simply is such a thing as a middle ear, and if its function is disturbed you can lose your balance."

"Well I know, but she's only got two ears, she says—" He wanted to make us laugh at African logic.

I gave him his brandy, and I went to the kitchen and quickly turned on the gas under the meat and mixed the dressing with the salad, using my unwashed hands as I always do when there's nobody to see.

He heard me clattering about in there and when I came out with the tray, I said to his broad smile, "What is it now?" and he said, "That's what I like about white girls, so efficient. Everything goes just-like-that."

"Oh, I'm making a special effort," I said, putting the bread and salad and butter on the table.

"Oh, I'm appreciative," he came back.

I was in and out, and each time I came into the living room he was an audience; then he held the baboon, amused, I could see in his face, full of curiosity, feeling that he had put his hand on my life—"So you've been fixing the monkey, eh? You keep busy all the time."

"It's Bobo's—my son."

"Nice thing for a little boy," he said, stroking the fur with one finger.

"Not so little any more. Maybe too old for it, now."

"Man, I could play with a thing like that myself."

I don't know whether he's professionally affable or if he really experiences the airy, immediate response to his surroundings that he always shows. Sometimes, when his great eyes are steady with attention to what I'm saying, there's a flicker—just a hair's-breadth flicker—that makes me aware that he's thinking, fast, in his own language, about something else.

He said, smiling, holding me in the admiring, kidding gaze that I rather enjoy, "Can't you sit down and relax a while?" Much of his small talk is in the style of American films he has seen, but it fits quite naturally, just as the rather too hairy, too tweedy jacket he wore was all right, on him. The delicious scent of onions stewing in butter grew as we talked. I asked about the Basutoland elections, and we were both content to warm up on neutral ground, so to speak. Then we got on to the position of the South African refugees there. He began to complain of the restrictions placed upon them by the British administration, referring to it as "your English friends," and I protested—"*My* friends? Why my friends?—Though I pity the poor devils, having to deal with a pack of squabbling political refugees—" "A-ah, they play nicely along with the South African government, don't you worry," he said. "—Specially the PAC chaps," I said. Our voices rose and we were laughing. "Beating each other up between speeches!" But under the laughter—or using the laughter—he veered away from the subject, that was too closely related to his visits to Johannesburg, would perhaps lead us too quickly to a point he would judge when to reach. I know that he doesn't come to see me for nothing. There's always a reason. Though once at least (the last time he came) he's gone away again without my finding out what it was; something must have indicated to him that he wouldn't get whatever it was that he wanted, anyway. He's nobody's fool, young Luke.

It was about ten when we got down to the food—it was sizzling and succulent the way it never is when someone else serves it up behind doors. He wanted a beer, but I was out of it, and so he carried on with the brandy and I had the lovely wine to myself. A few years ago I would have protested; I've developed a secret, spinsterish (or is it bachelor) pleasure in such small selfish greeds. (I in my flat, I suppose, and Graham in his house.) While it went down, warm as the temperature of the room, black-red, matt as fresh milk on the back of my tongue, I thought of how once—long ago, at the beginning—I said to Max, what would one do if somebody you loved died, how did one know how to go on? I always remember what he said: Well, after even only a few hours, you get thirsty, and you want again—you want a drink of water. . . ."

The dinner was so awfully good. It was like a feast. I said to the man with the smooth black face and long eyes, opposite me, "I don't know whether you saw in the paper; my husband is dead." After I had spoken my heart suddenly whipped up very fast, as it does when you have got something out at last. And yet I hadn't thought about mentioning anything to this visitor; the day was over, it had no connection with the visit; the visit had no connection with anything else in my life, such visits are like the hour when you wake up in the night and read and smoke, and then go to sleep again—they have no context.

His mouth was full of food. He looked at me dismayed, as if he wanted to spit it out; I felt terribly embarrassed. "Christ, I didn't know. When was that?"

I said, "I've been divorced for ages, you know. I've had Bobo alone with me since he was quite small."

"The fellow in Cape Town—he was the one you were married to? I read about it but I—"

"Yes, I had a telegram early this morning. I hadn't seen him or heard from him for a year."

He kept saying, over again, "Good God . . . I didn't know, you see."

I went on eating in order to force him to do so, but he sat looking at me: "Hell, that's bad, man. So what did you do, Liz, what'd you do?"

I could feel him watching me while I ate, spearing a piece of meat, scooping a few soft rings of onion onto it, and putting the fork in my mouth. When I had finished that mouthful, I sat back a bit in my chair and looked at him. "There's nothing to do, Luke. I drove out to the school, that's all, to tell my son."

"What about the funeral?"

"Oh, that'll be in Cape Town." I wanted to bring the facts of life home to him, so to speak.

"So you're not going?" No doubt he was thinking of an African family funeral, with all feuds and estrangements forgotten, and everyone foregathering from distant and disparate lives.

"No, I won't be going."

"He *was* the husband," he said.

"Oh yes," I said, "I know that. I've been thinking, he must have been the one for me. It couldn't have been much different."

We size each other up entirely without malice. I don't pretend to know anything about him, except what I can pick up in his innocent, calculating, good-looking plump face, he interprets me entirely as an outsider—I the outsider—by the exigencies of the life he belongs to.

Slowly he began to eat again, we both went on eating, as if I had persuaded him to it. He said, "Wha'd'you think made him do it? Political reasons?" He knows, of course, that Max turned State witness, that time.

"If he'd been one of your chaps he wouldn't have needed to do it himself, ay?—someone else would have stuck a knife in him and thrown him in the harbour."

He said, "Hell, Liz, man, take it easy"—with a short snort of a laugh. But it's true; it's all so much simpler if you're black, even your guilt's dealt with for you. African State witnesses appear masked in court, but they can't count on lasting long.

"You think he couldn't get it off his mind?"

I said, "Oh I don't know, Luke, I really don't know."

"But, man, you knew him from way back, you knew what sort of person he was, even if you haven't seen him lately."

"He wasn't the sort of person he thought he was."

"Ah, well." He didn't want to risk speaking ill of the dead. I said, by way of comfort, "There are people who kill themselves because they can't bear not to live forever"—I smiled with my lips turned down, in case he thought I was talking about an afterlife in heaven—"I mean, they can't put up with the limitations of the time they're alive in. Saints and martyrs are the same sort." But he just said, "The poor chap, ay," and I had a glimpse of myself as another white woman who talks too much. I offered him wine again. "No, I'll stick to this," he said, so I filled up my own glass; drinks too much, too, I thought. But I was in a calm, steady mood, I never drink when I am in a bad one. We helped ourselves to more food, a to-and-fro of hands and dishes and no ceremony. He was telling me about Reba's scheme to build six freehold houses for better-off Africans round the Basutoland capital. "If Reba could only get someone to back him, he could really go ahead. He can get cheap bricks and cheap timber—"

"But what sort of houses will they be!"

"No, they're all right. Reba knows what he's doing. Did you ever know that fellow Basil Katz? Yes, he's up there now and he's done some drawings and everything for Reba."

I wasn't much interested, and it was easy to sound sympathetic. "The building societies won't play?"

"No, man, of course not, they won't do it for a black. It's a shame. I'm sorry for Reba, he's dead keen and he knows he can get the cement and the bricks and the timber— cheap, really cheap. And he's got the labour—you know, it's a good thing to show the Basutos you're providing employment—it's a good thing."

"I don't suppose he can offer enough security—what's it?"

"—Collateral. Yes, that's it. But if he was a white, it'd be a different story—" Talking business, he assumed, perhaps unconsciously, the manner that he thought appropriate, chair tipped back, body eased casually. "On, say, thirty thousand rand, reckoning on a return of ten per cent—well, call it eight—you can expect a profit of close to three thousand, d'you realize that?"

"But is there anyone there to buy houses like that? Have they got the money—I mean I should have thought it would have to be a subeconomic scheme of some kind."

"They've got it, they've got it. And Reba knows how to get it out of them." He spoke with the city man's contempt for country people. "Reba's in with the Chiefs, man. You should see the cattle they've got. Not the poor devils up in the mountains! Reba goes and sits and drinks beer with them, and talks and talks, man, and he tells them how when independence comes the new African government's going to need houses for the ministers and people, in the town . . . he t-a-l-k-s to them . . ." Breaking into Sotho, he showed me Reba palavering with the yokels—watching, with a white flick of his long eyes, my laughter. I wondered what he was putting up the performance for; what he had come for. But I had forgotten about this at the moment when I said, "And that's what you're doing in Johannesburg, trying to raise money for the tycoon's houses"—and neatly gave away to him the opening he wanted.

He looked at the piece of cheese he had just taken and pushed it away with the knife and got up, turning from the table. His full belly in the white shirt strained over his belt and he lifted it, expanding his chest in a deep breath. When he spoke again it was from another part of his mind: "No"—softly, stiffly, as if it were none of my business— "No . . . not houses. That's . . . that's Reba's"—his hand made a loose, twirling gesture.

"What d'you do—for a living, Luke?" I came and stood

in front of him with my arms folded. (He had told me that he was once a salesman for ladies' underwear, in the townships.)

What a face, those extraordinary cloisonné eyes, you could put your finger on the eyeball to try the smooth surface. His chin lifted, to parry me, yet the smile, innocently blatant, would not be held back. The eyes filmed over as if someone had breathed on them. He grinned.

"Oh, I know; you're not the sort of person one can ask that."

"I'm with Reba—you know—" He was laughing, fumbling.

"No, no—I know you're fully occupied, but how do you *live?* Haven't you got a family somewhere?"

"Not me. I travel solo." It's taken for granted that we both know there's a wife and children. He's an expert at conveying what one might call sexual regret: the compliment of suggesting that he would like to make love to you, if time and place and the demands of two lives were different. I suppose he's found that this goes down very well with the sort of white women who get to know black men like him; they feel titillated and yet safe, at the same time. In sounding for the right note to strike, with me, he naturally tries this out among other things; I can't very well tell him that I've had a black lover, years ago. He trailed the tips of his fingers along my ear and down my neck; a good move, if he'd only known it—I particularly like the rosy, almost translucent pads on the inner side of black hands, that look as if light were cupped in them.

He put his arms round me and mine went round his warm, solid waist. We rocked gently. I teased him; "I sup-

pose you're supported by the Communist Party"—like all
PAC people, he accuses the ANC of being led by the nose,
first by Moscow and then by Peking.

"That's right, that's it." And, laughing, we broke away
and drifted round the room, he saying, "I admit everything . . . I confess," and I bringing over our cups of
coffee. He settled awkwardly, on a stool that was too low for
him, legs bent apart at the knees. I took my corner of the
sofa. "It's nice to be here," he said. "This room. I run all
around through this dirty town—ever since Wednesday—
and then this room. My, I remember the first night—you in
your nightie, with a little red—red, was it? Red with just a
li-ttle bit of a pattern, here and there—" (my raw silk gown
that I don't usually wear, because you can't wash the thing,
but I put it on if someone turns up and I'm not dressed)
"—but you came to the door calm as anything, not afraid at
all of the two strange blacks on your doorstep."

Was it money? Sometimes he pays back and sometimes he
doesn't; I couldn't remember whether he owes me anything
at present. "I knew Reba," I put in, from my vantage on
the comfortable sofa, not to make it too easy for him. "I'd
seen Reba before."

"But you didn't know who it was. You didn't recognize
him, I saw it. And you politely asked us in, just the
same"—a bit of business here—"and I even got a scrap of
cold food from your supper . . . Liz . . ." He was smil-
ingly reproaching me, in flattery, for my good nature.
"Lizzie . . ." The play on my name, using incongruously,
intentionally clumsily and quaintly, the form in which it is
the kitchen girl's generic, made a love-name of it.

"I just didn't know what else to say," I said flippantly,
and caught again behind his eyes the recording of a piece of

intelligence in words I did not know: he was encouraged to hope again, this time, I shouldn't know what to say, and again I'd simply be bewildered into giving what was wanted of me.

He shifted heavily on the low seat and screwed up his eyes with a distressed movement of his head, as if someone were shining a light on him. It was a kind of pantomime of despair—for my benefit. He drew breath to speak, and then caught it up short, and let his hands express the attempt in a limp jerk. And yet behind the show he was putting on there was for me something real that he wasn't aware of— the sense of this young black bull in the white china shop, with its nice little dinners and bookshelves and bric-à-brac and coffee-cup talk.

"These few days," he said, "I've racked my brains . . . these few days! Morning to night, going here and going there. I'm telling you, it's been a time . . ."

I said nothing, but waited, and he picked up the cue. "You see, if we're going to keep anything alive, if we're going to look after the chaps—there's lawyers to pay all the time—now all these cases in the Eastern Cape—"

He drew me in with a look, and I nodded; twenty-one PAC men were charged with sabotage this week—it was a small mention in the paper, there are so many of these cases, all people who were detained a year ago and are only now beginning to be charged.

"But doesn't Defence and Aid provide lawyers?" Always the orderly white mind, accustomed to dealing with disaster through the proper professional channels.

He put up a hand as if to say, not so fast. "They do, they do, to a certain extent—but you know how it is, there're all sorts of snags, man. You know how these things are; it's all got to be cut and dried and investigated and approved. And it's not only legal defence you've got to worry about. It's the families and so on." He looked straight at me for a moment with calm, oval eyes from which all communication seemed to slide wide away. "There are other problems." He saw nothing, while a fact was laid swiftly under my gaze.

I said, "I know so little these days. I have to believe what the papers say, there's nothing going on in the townships, the underground's broken for the time being."

"That's right," he said, "That's all you know, Liz, that's all you need to know." He was flattering again. He knows we whites love to feel we are "all right," to be trusted; and sufficiently "in" to understand an unspoken confidence.

He said suddenly, "You remember Colonel Gaisford, hey?" and I laughed and was about to say, God, that poor old codger—but it was a good thing I didn't, because he went on—"He was a grand old man, one of the best, a good friend to us, a true friend"—the sort of missionary phraseology that the Colonel himself might have used. Colonel Gaisford was a man whose kind of goodness becomes naïveté in a situation whose realities he doesn't understand. He went to jail last year, protesting quite truthfully that he didn't know that the money in the charitable fund he was administering was being used to send people out of the country for military training. But I saw that Luke's feeling for the old man, the man they used quite shamelessly, was genuine, and the hearty epithets were the only ones he had to convey a sense of nobility. "I'm telling you, you can't replace a man like that. I mean we've had a few people helping us since then"—he delicately mentioned one or two names; and now I had heard them, now I was aware of being drawn still further in—"but it hasn't worked out too well."

It was a curious way of putting it; one of the names has fled the country, another, of course, is under house arrest. In fact, that was the very difficulty he was coming to—"He's under house arrest and it's pretty impossible for him to handle the money."

"There's still money coming into the country?"

It wasn't a matter for my curiosity, but he had drawn me along so far, and I suppose he felt he owed me something. "Coming in, all right. At least it would if we could arrange for it. Good God, Liz, if you knew what I've tried, these few days. I've been battling to fix something up, but wherever I go, from this one to that one, there's a snag—"

"It's dangerous! Don't you think they know about you, by now?"

He didn't answer, only smiled as if to say, debonairly, let's leave that one alone. If he hasn't someone on his tail, he would never admit it, and if he has, well, the fact has long since been accepted by both trailed and trailer, they will run their course together.

"It's such an easy thing, too, Liz man"—as if I could banish the obtuseness, the unwillingness of "this one and that one"—"it's just somebody with a bank account with a bit of money in it. Somebody who gets cash from overseas sometimes—that's all you need. Don't you know someone who'll take a few extra credits for the next few months?"

So that was it. I was caught out; like that game we used to play as children, when the one who was "he" would drop a handkerchief behind your back and you would suddenly find yourself "on"; it doesn't matter how alert you think you're being, you still get the handkerchief served on you.

There was a quickening of wits between us. "Who on earth would I know!" I made it sound ridiculous.

"Some friend—" If I had drawn back, he had stepped up to confront me. He had that expression again, as if the sun were in his eyes: dazzled but not deflected.

"But what friend?"

His large eyes took in, barred in advance, any way out I might try. He waited.

"I don't know anybody—and what about the Colonel?" Anyone who received this money would go the same way as old Gaisford.

"No, there's no chance of that—we've got it taped, now." He gave the fatally easy assurance you always get from people like him. "And we won't use one account for more than six months or so, from now on."

He went on looking at me, half-smiling, satisfied I couldn't get away.

"You're not thinking of me!"

It was absurd, but he saw the absurdity as another attempt at evasion, and made me feel as if I were concealing something by it. But what? It's true that I have no money coming to me from abroad, in fact nothing in the bank more than the small margin—which often dwindles into the red—between the salary I deposit at the beginning of a month and the bills I pay by the end. He laughed with me, at last, but beneath it, I saw his purpose remain; the laughter was an aside.

"Ah, come on, Liz."

I told him he must be mad. I didn't know of anyone,

anyone at all whom I could even approach. I said I was out of that sort of circle long ago—a meaningless thing to say since we both knew he wouldn't have come to me, couldn't have come to me, otherwise. But everything I was saying was meaningless. What I was really telling him and what he understood was that I should be afraid to do what he asked, should be afraid even if I knew "someone," even if I had some feasible explanation for money suddenly coming into my bank account. We kept up the talk on a purely practical level, and it was a game that both of us understood—like the holding and flirting. The flirting is even part of this other game; there was a sexual undertone to his wheedling, cajoling, challenging confrontation of me, and that's all right, that's honest enough.

I said I'd think about it; I'd try and come up with a suggestion. If I could think of someone, I'd perhaps even sound out whoever it was, to see. He told me a few more details— "Just let me brief you" (he likes that sort of phrase)—as if the person would ever exist.

And while we talked, the thought was growing inside me, almost like sexual tumescence, and like it—I was nervous —perhaps communicating its tension: there's my grandmother's account. She has always had dividends coming in from all over the place. For more than a year, now, in order to make payments (for the Home, and other odd expenses) independent of her unreliable mental state, I have had her power of attorney. I was afraid Luke would somehow divine—not the actual fact, but that there was a *possibility;* that there really was something for me to conceal. His hand, his young, clumsy presence (there at my pleasure, I could ask him to leave whenever I wanted) hung over it. And at the same time I had the feeling that he had somehow known all along, all evening, that there was a possibility, some hidden factor, that he would get me to admit to myself. Probably just the black's sense that whites, who have held the power so long, always retain somewhere, even if they have been disinherited, some forgotten re-source—a family trinket coming down from generations of piled-up possessions.

"Even for say six months, good God, you don't know how important it would be for us—even just a few months." We went on talking as though the nonexistent "someone" I should never approach were already found.

I kept saying, "Well, I can't promise anything—maybe as I think about it . . . there might be a name I can't think of straight off. But I doubt it. . . ." and he hovered on the margin of my uncertainties and excuses, snapping them up like a bird swooping on mosquitoes: "It'd be marvellous, man. Our hands are tied, tied! The money's there in Lon-don, waiting for us, but for eight months now—eight months!—we haven't been able to move, our hands are tied!"

"Well, I'll look around and let you know."

"You'll let me know?"

I said, yes, we'd be in touch; we always say that when he comes; it means that perhaps in six weeks, three months, he will turn up again, and I'll tell him that I'm awfully sorry, I couldn't find anyone.

He said, "Tomorrow night?"

But I could say with a laugh at his impatience, "It's to-morrow already—give me a chance. I'll have to think."

So he said, affectionately, watchfully, "All right, Tuesday or Wednesday, maybe. You see I've got to get back, I can't hang around here too long." He kept looking at me with a jaunty, admiring male pride, as if I were displaying some special audacity that charmed him. "I'd better let you get some sleep," he said, coming over and putting out a hand to pull me up from the sofa. I was chilly and wrapped my arms round myself. "What'll you do now"—his eyes took in the room again—"phone the boy-friend?" I looked at him and smiled. "He's fast asleep long ago." We spoke softly at the door, and, when I opened it, signalled good night, because of the light still showing behind the glass door of the flat opposite. The soles of his shoes creaked, and I wanted to laugh. He grinned and, with just the right, light regret, put the palm of his hand a moment on my backside, with the gesture with which one says, wait there.

And so he's gone, my Orpheus in his too-fashionable jacket, back to the crowded company that awaits him somewhere in the town-outside-the-town. In a way it must be a relief to leave behind pale Eurydice and her musty secrets, her life-insured Shades (Graham has made me take out an all-risk policy). At this time of night, all the objects in the room lie around me like papers the wind has blown flat in an empty lot. I stand about; but where can I go, to whom? This is the place I have hollowed out for myself. Only the flowers, that are opening their buds in water and will be dead by Monday, breathe in the room. I put my face in among them, ether-cool snowdrops; but it is a half-theatrical gesture.

I even thought I might go out for a while, go down to one of the Hillbrow clubs where people I know are likely to be on a Saturday night. I do that, sometimes, when Graham has gone home. I put on a coat and some lipstick and go to one of those noisy dark places he's never seen the inside of. He talks about "the white laager" but this is really it, in a way: all the German and Italian immigrant men, looking for the street-life of Europe, and the young white South Africans and their girls, playing at low life, while outside in the lanes the black prostitutes and male transvestites hang about for whose who are serious. In some of these places there are lean young men with guitars, and you hear everyone join in the singing of "We Shall Overcome," just as if it were "My Bonny Lies over the Ocean." I ought to take Graham there sometime. But that would be an encroachment on my private life.

I have left everything in the room as it was—the onion-rings congealed on our plates, Luke's table-napkin thrown on the floor when he turned away from the table, the cheese for the mice to climb up and get at, the monkey lying on the sofa. Tomorrow, for an extra half-crown, Samson will clean it all up and take away the left-overs in an old jam tin. I cream my face as I do every night, as a man carefully cleans and oils his gun after use. I lie in bed, in the dark, and my body follows the routine ritual preparation for sleep: left side with right leg drawn up; belly-down, head to left; left leg drawn up, head to right, weight slowly given to the right side.

Perhaps he's talking now in the language I don't understand, full of exclamations and pauses for emphasis, telling them he's found a white woman who'll do it. But that's nonsense, there's no possible way he can know about my grandmother's account. It's not written on my forehead. He's gone. In three or four months' time he'll turn up again, and it'll be as if the whole thing has been resolved. Africans are instinctively tactful in these matters. He knows that all my talk about trying to think of someone, asking for time, etc., is just a face-saving way—for him and me—of saying no. He knows it. He must know it well. And next time he'll want something else from me, a fiver again perhaps, or even just a meal, and it won't be expedient to bring up what he asked for the last time.

The headlights of a car making the steep turn into the street send a great pale moth of light travelling slowly round the room; I turn on my back to follow it. Then there's darkness again, but some other light, a street-lamp perhaps, casts a wavering panel, spattered and blobbed (the shadow of the branch of a tree?) like the reflection of light in water. But water is heavy and dark, under its own weight, there's no light down there. I know they must have brought him up when they recovered the suitcase full of papers; but he'll always be down there, where he chose to go, where he had his last conscious thought. Max was dropped from the late final edition, crowded out by the astronauts. They are still up somewhere above my head. The moon, next time.

I should have kept the front page, with pictures, to send to Bobo. I must remember in the morning.

I don't know what time it is. Often you can tell from the quality of the darkness and silence whether you have wakened deep in the night, or towards morning. It can't be much before morning, I went to bed late and I seem to have come up from a long sleep. Yet it is quite dark and still, layer on layer of sleep suspended in the building between the earth and the open dark . . . and now, very far off, I heard quite distinctly the shuffle and clash of couplings falling into place between the coaches of a train; the railway yards are about two miles from here and one never knows they're there.

Since I've been awake I've been thinking very clearly. It's as if sediment has settled in my mind during sleep, and, like my hearing, all my faculties are perfectly acute. If I moved at all, the stir might produce cloudiness, as a snowstorm comes up in Bobo's paperweight; but all my muscles are in perfect tension, too, and I am not aware of what position I'm lying in. I'm clear as a fish in a lighted bowl, as their (silvery?) capsule up there in the empty night that stretches even further than the lilac goes. "From the Pacific to the Atlantic in twenty minutes"; when Max drowned today, a man walked about in space.

Why the moon?

There's no moon tonight, or else the room couldn't be so dark.

Isn't it the same old yearning for immortality, akin to all our desires to transcend all kinds of human limits? The feeling that if you bring such a thing off you're approaching the transcension of our limits of life: our death. We master our environment in order to stay alive, but this is mastery only over the human span, whether that's measured by three-score-and-ten or its prolongation for a few years—as with the old lady—by medicine. We've learnt how to stay alive—until it's time to die.

You can go down after love or up after the moon.

But if you master something *outside* our physical environment, isn't it reasonable to believe you are reaching out beyond the fact of death? If you master that beyond, as those men up there have done, isn't that the closest we've ever got to mastering death? Won't it seem the prefiguration, the symbol of that mastery?

They are alive, up there.

The very scene of operations is significant. We call the nothing above me "the sky"; and that way it's become the roof of our environment, part of our terrestrial and finite being, witness of our moment of eighty-seven years or thirty-one (he would have been thirty-two next month). But we know that that "nothing," beyond the layer of cloud I've seen for myself from a plane, that wrapping of atmosphere that others have soared above—that "nothing" is space. Twin of time, the phrase goes. I hear it in Graham's voice: together they represent, in the only conception we're capable of forming of it, infinity. Nightly, lilac infinity.

If that man over my head can get out of "the sky" into space, step from his man-devised, man-controlled casing into an environment beyond man's, move of his own volition into the vortex our planet was flung from and in which its cooling and bringing forth of life and the emergence of man and all his works together occupy (if you try to think of it in terms of time) a moment—if he can do this, can he really be still mortal? If God is the principle of the eternal, isn't he near God, tonight? Nearer than Max—who tried love—at the bottom of the sea. After all, religions teach that the kingdom of God, of the spirit, is not of this world. Flesh is of this world; death is of this world, but only by death we shall enter eternal life. Space is not of this world, either, and yet you can walk about alive in it, up there. You don't need to be dead in order to enter. Is there anything surprising that there should be a deep connection in our

subconscious between the eternity of God and the infinity
of space? In fact, some scientists set out to prove that these
are one and the same, and nearly all believe that there is
some identity, at least, between religious myths and the
evolutionary drive towards higher forms of life.

What's going on overhead is perhaps the spiritual expression of our age, and we don't recognize it. Space ex-
ploration isn't a "programme"—it's the new religion. Out
of the capsule, up there, out of this world in a way you can
never be, gone down to the seabed; out of this world into
infinity, eternality. Could any act of worship as we've
known such things for two thousand years express more
urgently a yearning for life beyond life—the yearning for
God?

That's what's up there, behind the horsing around and
the dehydrated hamburgers and the televised blood tests. If
it's the moon, that's why . . . that's why . . .

. . . there's no reason Luke shouldn't come back here.

I must have dropped off for a moment; I return with the
swoop of a swing towards the ground from the limit of its
half-arc.

The cheque book is in the left-hand upper drawer of my
dressing table. Not three feet away. It would be quite feasible for me to use my power of attorney over my grandmother's account. It is simply a matter of ascertaining (Graham's
word) exactly how I should deposit in her account cheques
from abroad; the procedure so far, with foreign exchange,
has been that if the currency is from outside the sterling
area, I fill in a form giving the source and nature of the
funds—dividends from shares in the such-and-such company and so on. And if the money is from the sterling area?

don't I have to state the source then, too? Well, of course, the payer's name has to be written on the ordinary desposit slip. That's routine. But what happens if the money is credited to the account by bank draft? As I remember it, there's some other sort of form to fill in, or was it that the source of funds had to be declared on the back of the transfer draft? It's happened once or twice, but I'm not sure what I did.

And what about income tax declaration. How do you get round that one? Well, Luke must have some ideas; he said that all that was needed was a bank account. Quite. Look at Colonel Gaisford.

Graham would be the one who would know exactly how one would stand with the bank and the income tax people; he would know exactly where and how one would be found out. This is one thing you could never ask Graham; this is the end of asking Graham. It was Graham who managed to make a successful application for a passport for me, last year, after I'd been refused one for years. Graham has defined the safe limits of what one can get away with—"a woman in your position."

There is certain to be some clause one'll fall foul of, some provision one can't fulfil. But for six months, even if it's only six months, he said—the bank account of an old woman, who will think of looking into that? My grandmother may only live another few months; it's as if the account exists for no other reason. She could never be held answerable for anything that might happen. But there's my signature, of course, the name Van Den Sandt. Yet by the time investigations are made about the source of money coming in, and the link is established with the destination of money being paid out . . . well, she may be dead, the account may no longer be being used for the same purpose. Everything is impossible, if one calculates on the safe side.

Why on earth should I do such a thing?

It seems to me that the answer is simply the bank account. I can't explain; but there is the bank account. That's good enough; as when Bobo used to answer a question about his behaviour with the single word: "Because." Am I going into politics again, then? And if so, what kind? But I can't be bothered with this sort of thing, it's irrelevant. The bank account is there. It can probably be used for this purpose. What happened, the old lady asked me: well, that's what's happened. Luke knows what he wants, and he knows who it is he must get it from. Of course he's right. A sympathetic white woman hasn't got anything to offer him— except the footing she keeps in the good old white Reserve of banks and privileges. And in return he comes with the smell of the smoke of braziers in his clothes. Oh yes, and it's quite possible he'll make love to me, next time or some time. That's part of the bargain. It's honest, too, like his vanity, his lies, the loans he doesn't pay back: it's all he's got to offer me. It would be better if I accepted gratefully, because then we shan't owe each other anything, each will have given what he has, and neither is to blame if one has more to give than the other. And in any case, perhaps I want it. I don't know. Perhaps it would be better than what I've had—or got. Suit me better, now. Who's to say it shouldn't be called love? You can't do more than give what you have.

It's so quiet I could almost believe I can hear the stars in their courses—a vibrant, infinitely high-pitched hum, what used to be referred to as "the music of the spheres." Probably it's the passage of the Americans, up there, making their own search, going round in the biggest circle of them all.

I've been lying awake a long time, now. There is no clock in the room since the red travelling clock that Bobo gave me went out of order, but the slow, even beats of my heart repeat to me, like a clock; afraid, alive, afraid, alive, afraid, alive . . .